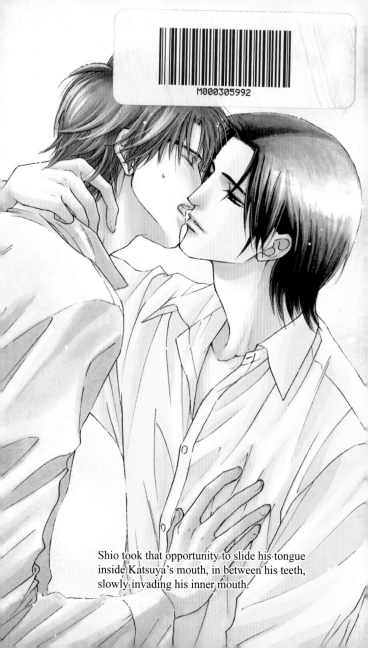

Shio took that opportunity to slide his tongue inside Katsuya's mouth, in between his teeth, slowly invading his inner mouth.

PROFILE

STORY

Yuuki Kousaka
Birthday: September 16th
Blood Type: B+

I found an "umaibo" (delicious stick) in my dad's car–it had been in there for a while. They're only 10 yen a piece, and I was amazed at how good it was for something so cheap. I'm really into these cheap delicious things right now. My mom thinks it's funny that I'm so easily pleased.

ILLUSTRATION

Midori Shena
Birthday: March 29th
Blood Type: O+

My recent goal has been to pass the expert level kanji exam. I kind of decided on a whim though. It's not really like it's going to help me in the future...

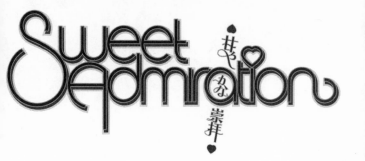

Sweet Admiration

甘やかな崇拝

Written by
YUUKI KOUSAKA

Illustrations by
MIDORI SHENA

English translation by
Andria Cheng

June
Los Angeles

OAKLA
PUBLISHING
Tokyo

SWEET ADMIRATION

Written by Yuuki Kousaka
Illustrated by Midori Shena
English translation by Andria Cheng

Co-Publishers:
Masahiro Nagashima – Oakla Publishing, Inc.
Hikaru Sasahara – Digital Manga, Inc.

English Edition Co-Published by:
OAKLA PUBLISHING
1-18-6 Kamimeguro
Meguro-ku, Tokyo 153-0051
Japan
www.oakla.com

DIGITAL MANGA PUBLISHING
A division of DIGITAL MANGA, Inc.
1487 W 178th Street, Suite 300
Gardena, CA 90248
USA
www.dmpbooks.com
www.junemanga.com

Library of Congress Cataloging-in-Publication Data Available Upon Request

First Edition: March 2008
ISBN-13: 978-1-56970-732-6
10 9 8 7 6 5 4 3 2 1

Printed in China

Sweet Admiration

甘やかな崇拝

Other novels published by
JUNÉ

Only The Ring Finger Knows vol.1
The Lonely Ring Finger

Don't Worry Mama

The Man Who Doesn't
Take Off His Clothes vol.1-2

Cold Sleep

Little Darling

Ai No Kusabi – The Space Between
Vol.1- Stranger

Body Language

Contents

Chapter 1

Ever since he was little, Katsuya had longed for certain moments: a mother who would show up at school, all dressed up for Parents Visiting Day; a mother, with an umbrella in hand, who would pick him up from school on days when it would start to rain suddenly; a mother who would call out, "It's getting late, time to come home!" or "Time for dinner, come inside!" when he'd play outside with his friends.

Ordinary moments between a mother and son.

But no matter how much Katsuya had longed for those moments, he could never have them.

Even if there had been pouring rain or a blizzard outside, Katsuya's mother had never picked him up from school. Some kind of work had always come up suddenly, so she had never even been able to come to Parents Visiting Day, or any sports meets he had looked forward to.

But even as a child, Katsuya had understood that his parents were both busy and didn't have much free time to spend with him. However, he had never once doubted their love for him. So he had never been selfish enough to say things like, "Come to Parents Visiting Day!" or "Bring an umbrella and pick me up from school on rainy days!"

On Parents Visiting Day, he had tolerated it

when his parents couldn't come, and on rainy days, he had used an umbrella from school. Katsuya had been a very obedient kid, and had been very good at coming home right before darkness fell whenever he played outside. In other words, he had been a good, obedient child who didn't have to be told to behave.

But still, there were some things he couldn't get used to.

When he had played over at friends' houses, their moms would bake cakes for them, and if it got too late, they would drive him home. Katsuya had thought it must be nice to have a mom who was always home to take care of her kids and to bake things for them.

But in reality, his parents had been too busy trying to pay off the loan on their new house. His parents had wanted to build the house so Katsuya could have his own room, so there had been no way he could complain.

Eventually, even though he was still a child, Katsuya had begun to accept that his friends' families had their own way of living, and his family had theirs. There were plenty of other kids like him, and there would always be people better off than him. He had decided he would just count his blessings.

* * *

In the lounge of a hotel bar somewhere in Tokyo, Katsuya Narita sat alone at a window side table with a nervous look on his face.

He wasn't a child anymore.

He had graduated from a national university in

spring, and had just found work at a company in Tokyo in April. It was the first time he had left home, the first time he had been to Tokyo; he had nothing but first experiences and nervousness as his time unfolded there. He had just arrived four days earlier.

He was supposed to live in a company housing and had arrived a few days before company orientation, because he figured there would be a lot of moving preparations to be made. However, his company wasn't ready for him yet, so he had had no choice but to stay in a hotel for now.

He had completed the company orientation, but with the housing issue still up in the air, it had put a damper on his fresh start in "the real world."

Katsuya Narita, 22 years old. Current residence: some city hotel.

He had just arrived in Tokyo and was already uneasy about his new lifestyle, thanks to this situation.

He needed a friend.

But Katsuya had lived in his hometown his whole life, so he didn't have many friends in Tokyo. He had promised to meet a friend from elementary school, Kazuki Ozawa, at the hotel lounge that night. Well, saying "a friend from elementary school" was a bit of an overstatement, because they had actually only spent one summer together in fourth grade.

Kazuki's family lived in Tokyo, but that summer, he had come to visit his uncle who lived in the same rural neighborhood as Katsuya. Kazuki had been the typical city kid, and had known all about the latest games and anime. But Katsuya had known lots of stuff

Kazuki didn't know. Like how to catch crawfish in the river, catch and raise beetles, climb trees, and where to find the best nuts and nectar...

They had become fast friends and played together from morning until night all summer long. But when the summer had ended, Kazuki had returned to Tokyo and, soon after, his uncle had passed away, so he hadn't come back to the country again. However, they kept in touch through letters and phone calls, so they had remained friends.

Kazuki was more than surprised when he received a call from Katsuya the day before, telling him he had found work in Tokyo and was already there.

Well, it's no wonder he was so surprised, Katsuya thought.

Kazuki had tried to get him to come to Tokyo for both high school and college. However, Katsuya had always said no, saying local schools were enough for him, and had even told Kazuki last year on the phone that he planned to look for work in his hometown.

Honestly speaking, he himself couldn't even believe that he was actually here in Tokyo. He had planned to find work back home and live out a simple life in the country. Never in his wildest dreams had he imagined going to work and living in Tokyo. Katsuya wondered if a sheltered, country boy like him could survive in the big city. However, he had come this far, he couldn't turn back now.

Kazuki sure is late...

As he sipped his cold coffee, Katsuya gazed out the window at the illuminated garden.

Kazuki had promised to meet him at 8:00 p.m. in the hotel lounge. There was still no sign of him, and it was already half-past eight. Katsuya had told a hotel employee his name and that he was expecting a guest, but it didn't seem like anyone was making any movement towards him.

Katsuya rested his chin in his hands and lost himself in thought.

It had been 12 years since he had last seen Kazuki...

We were both children back then, and we've grown up so much, we might not even recognize each other...

Katsuya was almost 180 centimeters tall now. His body had grown muscular from always having played sports, and he was proud of his well-toned physique. He had been thin as a rail when he was a kid, so it was possible that Kazuki wouldn't recognize him. Similarly, Katsuya wasn't confident he'd be able to spot Kazuki, either.

Katsuya still couldn't believe he had graduated from college and was now a member of society.

However, not only had Kazuki failed his college entrance exams, but he had had to repeat a year of school, so even though they were the same age, he was only a sophomore now. Whenever he had free time, he liked to take random trips around the country. Not only had he hiked all around Japan, but last year, he had even been to Australia.

Kazuki's actions always managed to surprise him. Katsuya, who was serious and conservative, could never understand what Kazuki was thinking. Maybe it was because they had such different personalities that he felt so drawn to Kazuki, and felt so stimulated by his friend.

While he thought about Kazuki, he suddenly remembered someone else's face. As usual, when he thought of this person, his mind became kind of fuzzy. He felt uneasy and sad for some reason. He didn't understand why he had these feelings, which he always kept hidden deep within himself.

That person was also a part of Katsuya's memories of his summer with Kazuki.

It was Kazuki's older brother, Shio.

He was four years older than them and had been in middle school at the time. The two siblings had come to visit their uncle together. Unlike Kazuki, who had immediately befriended Katsuya and gotten all muddy running around with him outside, the slender, fair-skinned Shio barely left their uncle's house.

According to Kazuki, Shio was always inside reading books, so Katsuya didn't see him very much. His only memories of Shio were of him colored by the setting sun. Kazuki and Katsuya would play together all day, running around even when they were covered in dirt. Every evening, Shio would come to get Kazuki. "Kazuki, it's getting dark, so you need to come home!" His white skin would always be a little sweaty, probably from searching all around for them.

"No way! I wanna play more!"

While scolding his little brother, Shio would look at Kazuya. "You, too. Your mom will worry if it gets too late."

His parents would always come home late from work, so there was no reason why they would be worried about him. But hearing Shio say that almost made Katsuya believe that someone *would* worry if he didn't get home soon.

Usually, with Shio's prodding, they would walk back home together. As the darkness drew nearer, the three of them would walk side by side down the country road, while Kazuki excitedly told his brother about the day's adventures.

"Uh-huh, uh-huh." Shio would listen to his younger brother patiently. Katsuya, trotting along beside them, would quietly gaze up at Shio's face, mesmerized by his clean-cut profile.

From the first time he had seen the other boy, he had always thought Shio was a very beautiful person. He had sensed that it was strange to have such feelings towards another boy, but that was genuinely how he felt; he couldn't help it.

How could he explain it? He couldn't describe him in just one word like "refined." It was *more* than that. Like, Shio had a certain urban feel to him that Katsuya had never experienced before in the country.

Around there, most middle school and high school students had worn their hair so short it was practically shaved. However, Shio's long, chestnut-colored hair had been smooth and silky; his facial features had been so beautiful one might almost mistake him for a girl.

When Katsuya had first met Shio, he had been completely awed by him, and his fascination deepened every time he would come to get Kazuki.

He had even mentioned it to Kazuki once. "Hey, your brother's a really beautiful person, don't you think so?"

Kazuki had answered breezily, "Really? I can't tell. But everyone always says he resembles Mom, so maybe that's why. People say I look like my dad, but I can't tell that either."

Katsuya hadn't understood why Kazuki couldn't see how beautiful his brother was, so much so that he had started to seriously wonder if there were so many beautiful people in Tokyo that Kazuki had simply become immune to beauty.

Shio-san...

Twelve years had passed since then.

Just as the once scrawny Katsuya had grown into a strong young man, the beautiful Shio must have grown up to be an amazing man. As he thought about Shio, his heart began to pound in his chest. Even though he was here to meet Kazuki, Katsuya began to feel like he was waiting for Shio.

And Kazuki still hadn't shown up.

What on earth is going on? Katsuya thought, as he checked his watch for the umpteenth time. Just then, he noticed a man walking briskly toward his table.

He was wearing a casual shirt and jeans, and his shiny brown hair was styled messily. As he met Katsuya's gaze, he raised his hand and said, "Hey!"

It was Kazuki. Even though it had been 12 years, Katsuya recognized him immediately.

"Kazuki!"

"Katsuya, it's been a long time, huh? I'm sorry I kept you waiting. I had a few things I had to take care of first."

Katsuya stood up excitedly, and they both looked each other over.

Kazuki's skin was golden brown from the sun and he showed white teeth when he smiled. Even though he looked like every other college student nowadays, his smile was definitely that of Katsuya's childhood friend. They exchanged a firm handshake.

"Oh, don't worry about it. Did you recognize me right away?" Katsuya asked.

"Of course!" Kazuki replied. "You haven't changed one bit, Katsuya."

"Really? It might be weird to say it myself, but I feel like I've changed a lot," Katsuya said, grinning as he invited Kazuki to sit, and then sat back down himself. They ordered drinks from the waiter, and then he gave Kazuki a nostalgic look.

"No way! You haven't changed at all," Kazuki said. "You still feel the same to me as you did back then. You definitely look more grown up, though. And now you're all muscular. But you're still you."

Katsuya felt kind of flattered. It made him strangely happy to hear an old friend tell him that he hadn't changed at all.

"You haven't changed much either, Kazuki. I recognized you right away."

Kazuki laughed. "Oh, so you're saying I haven't grown up much, right?"

That might be true, but Kazuki was probably 175

centimeters tall now. He was still as thin as ever, but his arms, peeking out from the sleeves of his shirt, were surprisingly muscular, probably from all the outdoor activities he enjoyed.

"Anyway, I was totally surprised when you called me! Didn't you tell me before that you had found work in your hometown? At some bank or brokerage firm or something?" Kazuki asked.

Katsuya nodded. "Oh, yeah. It wasn't official, though. I ended up deciding on somewhere else, which is why I came to Tokyo."

"Don't act like it's no big deal!" Kazuki said. "I've been asking you for years to come to Tokyo and you never wanted any part of it! So why now? Did something happen that changed your mind?"

"No, not exactly," Katsuya answered.

"I don't think you'd do a complete 180 degree-turn without a good reason," Kazuki insisted. "You've always been determined to stay in your hometown and stick to the straight and narrow."

Even though they had just met for the first time in 12 years, Kazuki was still straightforward, getting right to the point. He'd always been very outspoken—that hadn't changed much.

"Well, I just thought it might not be a bad idea to have an adventure out here, is all. It seemed kind of sad to only know my hometown. So I thought if I was going to move to the city, now would be the best time."

"Exactly! That's what I've been telling you! You should've come to a famous private university in the city to begin with! The universities here are fun,

Katsuya! There are tons of pretty girls and group dates are constantly going on. You could have *any* cute girl you want here!"

"Nah. Unlike you, I didn't go to college just to hit on girls." A bitter smile spread unintentionally across Katsuya's face. He was reminded of Kazuki's speeches when trying to persuade him to come to Tokyo for college. He would always say, "You'd be really popular with the ladies, so you gotta come!"

He took a breath as the waiter brought over the drinks.

Kazuki drank half of his iced tea in one gulp, and said, as if he was just remembering it, "Oh, yeah. You haven't told me what company you'll be working for yet. What is it?"

"Uhh..." Katsuya hesitated.

"You turned down that other job and came all the way here for it, so it must be pretty good. What is it, a television station? Newspaper? A famous publishing company or something?"

"No, it's actually a newly-formed IT company..."

"Oh, IT companies are great. It's really a cutting-edge field right now. Depending on how well it keeps up with the times, you could have a huge success story there. So which IT company is it?" Kazuki leaned forward excitedly.

Katsuya had been expecting him to ask that, but now that it was really happening, he wasn't sure how to answer. He figured that if he came right out and said it, Kazuki would be extremely surprised. But his reaction *after* his surprise was what Katsuya was afraid of, so he was hesitant to answer. But he knew he had to, so he prepared himself for the worst. Even if he didn't tell him now, Kazuki would find out eventually, so he might as well just put himself at ease as soon as possible.

"Slice City Corporation."

"What?" Kazuki stared at him blankly.

Maybe he didn't hear me, Katsuya thought, and repeated himself. "I'm going to work at Slice City Corporation."

"...Why?" Kazuki tilted his head to one side strangely, as if he didn't understand what Katsuya was saying. Somehow, it seemed like his answer had far exceeded what Kazuki had been expecting.

"What do you mean, why? Just...because."

"...Uhh, but I was the one who told you about that company, right?"

"Yeah..."

It was true that Katsuya had heard about the company from him during a phone call last year. Kazuki had probably just intended to simply inform him about it, but...

"Did you decide to work there because I told you about it?" Kazuki asked.

"Well, I guess you could say that," Katsuya answered.

"But that company only started last year. No one has any idea whether it'll be a success or a total failure! Choosing a company like that is an awfully big gamble."

"Really? I hadn't heard about all that."

So it was a risky move to go with that company,

Katsuya thought. The image of the office he had just joined rose to the back of his mind. A small building in Kandasurudagai. It was a cozy little office, encircled by cabinets, desks and chairs that were still new. With only 20 employees, it was a small company. It had just been started the year before, apparently a "gamble," as Kazuki had said.

Well, no matter what he said, I've already been hired, so it's too late now, Katsuya thought.

It seemed like Kazuki was starting to piece the details together. With a confused look, he cautiously watched Katsuya's face, asking, "Could it be that...you joined the company because I told you my brother started it?"

"Well...I didn't think about it right away. But I had been wondering how Shio-san was doing, what his company was like. So I looked up the company's number and gave them a call. Apparently, they had just started to accept job applications, so they mistook me for an applicant. Before I knew it, I had agreed to take the employment test..."

"So, you came all the way to Tokyo to take it?"

"No, when I told them where I lived, they arranged for someone to come give me the test and interview there."

"Wow. I can't believe the company came all the way to you!"

"Since they used their travel expenses to come give me the test, I couldn't really refuse them. They were really enthusiastic and insistent, so that's how I ended up getting hired."

"Well, since they're such a new IT company, they probably thought the most they could hope for were some laid-back students from a third-rate university. I'm sure they went out of their way for someone like you who was an excellent student from a national university."

Well, they didn't really go out of their way, but Katsuya had to admit that the company had been extremely eager to hire him. Besides that, he knew Shio would be there, so that was why Katsuya had decided on the company.

"Well, a lot happened, but now that I'm officially hired, I don't regret anything. I just think that you never know where the cards might fall."

"So, have you seen my brother yet?" Kazuki asked.

"No. I totally thought that Shio-san was the president, but I guess not. I already introduced myself to all the higher-ups, but I haven't seen him yet."

"I must have explained it wrong. He didn't actually start the company, but he's one of its investors. I'm sure he's some kind of executive, but he's involved in the establishment of lots of other companies, so he's probably always running around somewhere," Kazuki said apologetically.

"Oh, I see."

"I didn't know you were so concerned about my brother. If I had explained things better, maybe you wouldn't be in this situation now. I'm sorry. I'll get a hold of my brother and ask him to make sure you have a good life at the company." Kazuki bowed his head.

Katsuya had never seen Kazuki act or talk this

way, and began to feel flustered. "Wh-why are you apologizing? Knock it off, okay? This is the path I've decided on for myself, and I told you I have no regrets. Also...please don't mention anything about me to Shio-san. I don't want to have any kind of unfair advantage at the office. It would cause trouble for him, and it would feel like I just got the job because of connections. I don't like that."

"Okay, then. But once they know you're an acquaintance of my brother, they'll probably start treating you better at the office, anyway."

"I said I don't like that kind of stuff! Do you think that I picked the company because I had some kind of ulterior motive? Because I'd have an advantage if Shio-san was there?"

"No, I'm not saying that. All I'm saying is that you have to use everything you can!"

Katsuya would rather die than do that. He had always preferred things to be fair and square, trying to live a life that wouldn't bring him any shame. Having that kind of unwanted help would be nothing more than a disgrace to him. Not only that, but if he did ask for some kind of favor, he was afraid of how Shio would react.

"Anyway, don't mention one word about me to Shio-san," he said in a firm voice.

Kazuki, looking as if he had relented, shrugged his shoulders in exasperation. "Looks like you're still stubborn as ever."

"Was I stubborn before?"

"You've always hated anything underhanded

ever since we were kids. You had such a one-track mind it was almost shocking. You were *totally* stubborn." Kazuki grinned, and winked at him.

He had only spent one summer with his friend, but Katsuya felt like Kazuki almost knew him better than he knew himself.

"Well, if that's what you want, I won't say a word. It might be a small, risky company now, but even the most successful IT presidents from Roppongi Hills had to start from the ground-up, right? That means your company has the same chance, Katsuya."

"You're right. I'm not sure how to explain it...but I feel like I'm even more motivated *because* it's a small company. I'll be able to see the direct results of my work, and I can watch the company change right before my eyes. I feel like that's a lot more interesting than being just another cog in a huge company. So that's why I decided on this one." Even as he said this, Katsuya knew that Shio's presence in the company had a much greater influence on his decision than anything else. But he knew Kazuki wouldn't know what to say to that, so he decided to keep it to himself.

"Anyway, are you still living in a hotel? The company must really expect a lot of you if they put you up in this ritzy city hotel. They're totally going out of their way for you!" Kazuki said as he finished the rest of his iced tea.

At this, Katsuya remembered why he had asked Kazuki there in the first place, and sat up straighter in his chair.

"Actually, the company didn't really arrange this.

When I came to Tokyo, I thought I would stay in a hotel until things calmed down, so I asked at the airport and they recommended this place. I'm paying for it myself, but Tokyo's hotel rates are *really* expensive!"

"Yeah, they are. But at this city hotel, you're getting ripped off exactly like all the tourists! If you're going to live here, you'd better start looking for an apartment or a condo. You won't be able to relax if you have to go to work from a hotel every day."

"Well, when I had my interview, they told me I could live in a company housing. I really thought I'd be able to move in soon, and that I'd only have to stay in a hotel for one or two days. But they told me I have to wait because the company housing isn't ready yet for some reason."

"That's terrible! They reeled you in by promising company housing! If you let me tell on them to Shio, I'm sure he'll give them hell!"

Katsuya glared at him, and Kazuki answered by waving his hand back and forth as if to say, "Okay, okay!"

"Actually, that's the reason I asked you here tonight. I can't afford to stay in a hotel for much longer, and I can't look for an apartment because of the company housing thing. Kazuki! I'm really sorry to ask you this, but can you let me stay at your place for a while?" Katsuya placed both hands on the table and bowed his head deeply.

He was fully aware of how rude he was being; the gall of coming out of the blue to hit up a friend he hadn't seen in 12 years. But he was between a rock and a hard place, and with the company housing still up in the air, and the president asking him to make do until they were ready for him, Kazuki was the only one he could rely on.

Kazuki held his cigarette in his mouth, surprised at Katsuya suddenly bowing his head so emphatically to him. "Wow...are you in *that* much trouble?"

"I'm sorry. I just can't afford to pay for the hotel anymore. I know I shouldn't be asking a favor like this so suddenly."

"No, I don't mind. It's a really small one-room apartment, though. And it's kind of dirty."

He didn't care how small or dirty it was. Just as Katsuya's eyes began to gleam at the prospect, Kazuki continued. "But right now, my girlfriend's there. Well, not just *there*. We're living together. So, if you're okay with that..."

His girlfriend.

Kazuki had a girlfriend? That was the first time Katsuya had heard of it. Of course, he had known that Kazuki might have a girlfriend, but the situation had changed now that he knew Kazuki's girlfriend was living with him. In a one-room apartment, no less. He wondered if he would even be willing to stay there as both a freeloader *and* a third wheel.

He came to the conclusion that there was just no way.

"Okay, never mind then," he said.

"Don't be silly!" Kazuki exclaimed. "It might be crowded, but as long as we don't ask for too much, we should be okay."

"No, I can't impose on you if you're in that kind of situation."

"You wouldn't be imposing, don't be ridiculous! Aren't we friends?"

"Yes, but you have a person living with you, right? It wouldn't be fair to her if some guy she didn't know suddenly moved in to your cramped, one-room apartment."

As Katsuya said "it wouldn't be fair," Kazuki sighed and looked up at the ceiling. "Okay, but I can't just ignore the fact that you're in trouble...I got it! I'll start looking for a cheap business hotel, and you can stay there for the time being. How does that plan sound?"

Of course, any place he could find that was cheaper than here would be great.

"That would help a lot."

"All right, let's do that, then. I'll look on the internet and find a good place for you by tomorrow morning. A condo that rents out by the week might be cheaper, so I'll look for those, too. I'll make sure you have nothing to worry about when you check out tomorrow. Leave it to me!" Kazuki pounded his chest confidently.

"Thank you so much! I knew I could count on you, Kazuki," Katsuya said gratefully, realizing that Kazuki was the proverbial "friend-in-need" this time.

The only way I'll be able to "check out with no worries" like Kazuki put it, might be when the company housing is officially ready, Katsuya thought with a bitter smile.

Chapter 2

The day after he met up with his friend, Katsuya gathered up his personal effects and moved into a room at a cheap business hotel Kazuki had found for him.

Since Katsuya wasn't familiar yet with Tokyo's transportation system, he had wanted to stay somewhere close to his work. Luckily, the new hotel was so close, he could walk there. But it was a trade-off; the hotel itself was a world of difference from the previous one he had stayed in. In fact, it looked like a cheap, back-alley hotel.

The room was small and the walls and ceilings were covered with stains. The bed sheets were somewhat damp. However, Katsuya had briefly escaped from the economic danger that had been making him so nervous, and that night he fell right to sleep.

The next day, he walked to work.

The hotel didn't offer any breakfast service, so he bought some milk and some freshly baked bread from a bakery he found on the way. With his breakfast in hand, he headed towards the company.

"Good morning!" He entered the office and greeted everyone in a loud voice.

"M-morning!"

"Good morning!"

His co-workers, who were just beginning to

become familiar faces to him, greeted him in unison.

Katsuya was part of the Sales Department. He made his way to his desk in the corner of the office and sat down. He quickly opened the bread wrapper and started to eat his late breakfast when Hiromi Inada, a female co-worker from Human Resources, approached him.

"Narita-san, about the documents we needed...you left your current address blank."

Katsuya coughed, nearly choking on his bread. He quickly washed it down with some milk.

The document she held out was the one he was supposed to fill out at orientation, but since the company housing hadn't yet been finalized, he had left his current residence blank and turned it in anyway.

"I'm sorry, but I'm not sure where I'll be living yet," he said.

"Is that so? Well, I'm sorry, but you really have to fill it out. We use the current address printed on this document to report to the welfare program and for tax purposes."

"The president said the company housing isn't ready yet, so I don't have anywhere to go. Right now, I'm staying at a hotel. Plus, I'm paying for it myself, so I'm in a bind, too."

"You're coming to work from a hotel?" Hiromi tilted her head with a puzzled expression.

"Uh, yes."

"Um, okay. Well, just put down the hotel's address, then."

Is that really okay?

Pulling a receipt from his wallet, Katsuya copied the hotel's address. An unintentional sigh escaped from his lips.

After he finished eating his bread, he started to arrange the sales materials he had received the day before, when Yuusuke Hatanaka, also from the Sales Department, approached him.

A man in his early 30s, Hatanaka was going to be training Katsuya.

"Morning. You're here early, aren't you?"

"Good morning. I switched hotels, and this one is a lot closer. I can walk to work from this one; it's pretty convenient," Katsuya said cheerfully.

Hatanaka said in a surprised voice, "You're in a pretty good mood for someone who's being forced to pay for his own hotel!"

"Well, that has nothing to do with my work. But just as I thought, it's difficult to relax there, so I hope something happens with the company housing issue soon. By the way, do you live in a company housing, Hatanaka-san?"

"No, I live in a normal rental condo. The company gives me a little housing allowance...but I don't think many of our co-workers even live in company housing."

"Really?"

"I heard the manager of Systems Development lives in a company housing. A condo in Tokiwadai, I believe. And I think a bunch of executives live in condos rented out by the company. But as I said, those are the higher-ups. I've never heard of any regular workers living in company housing."

As soon as Katsuya heard this, he had a bad premonition. "Is that so...well, at both my interview and when he told me I got the job, the president said, 'Oh, we have company housing, so don't worry about where to live when you come to Tokyo!' all full of confidence and pounding on his chest."

"Well, he was probably exaggerating a little because he wanted someone of your talent so much. The president has built this company mostly on self-confidence and bluffs. But if he said to wait a little longer, why don't you try to wait a bit more? Someone of your talent has finally joined our company, so I don't think he'd let you get away. I'm sure something can be done."

Hatanaka said this in a carefree way, but Katsuya wasn't so sure.

A company founded mostly on confidence...and bluffs? Okay...

After all, the president, Soga, was only in his late 20s. He was one of the many young entrepreneurs in the industry. He had an athletic build and a strong, authoritative voice. He was always full of energy. When he heard about a good deal, he would go anywhere in Japan and was proud of his light footwork. At Katsuya's interview, he had been both persuasive and passionate. Katsuya had eventually been persuaded by that enthusiasm and decided to work for him.

Somehow...

Somehow, Katsuya felt like he just understood now the true meaning of what Kazuki had said earlier about it being a risky move to work for this company.

* * *

The company Katsuya had joined, Slice City, offered their clients various information collected from the internet. In other words, it was an information and communications company.

When it was first established, its main focus had been hosting and maintaining internet servers and website-related consultations. However, they had expanded their business affairs to include the administration of a portal site, called "Slice City," and multimedia planning and production.

Therefore, there were many development engineers and network engineers on the art staff, but the rest of the work was left up to the Sales Department, which Katsuya belonged to.

"While the art staff can relax and devote themselves to their work, we have to suck up to clients to secure jobs. If we didn't do that, this company wouldn't even exist. Our jobs are like being stage hands for some glamorous stage production. Without stage hands, it would be impossible to put on such a large show. This job is difficult sometimes, and it's easy to feel down when you get scolded for something. But that makes the sense of accomplishment even greater when you finally secure a contract. That's why I can't quit this job," Hatanaka said suddenly while they were on their way back to the office. They had just visited all their regular clients without securing a single advertisement, and were now totally exhausted.

Because the day's efforts had been in vain, Katsuya guessed Hatanaka, as his senior, felt he should give Katsuya some words of encouragement.

"Don't worry. I won't give up after just one day of strike-outs. Sales is all about the accumulation of each day's efforts," Katsuya said with a smile.

Hatanaka raised his eyebrow in surprise. "You said it better than I did."

"Both my mother and father were in sales. They often talked about work when they came home, and I also heard their complaints, so I'm fully aware of the hardships of this kind of work.

That's right.

Even though Katsuya never had a mother who would greet him at home everyday like he had so longed for when he was little, he had had a mother and father who worked hard. He was thankful now to his parents for showing him the hardships of business.

"Is that right? Well, I guess I spoke too soon. We're not like those large companies that have the time to spend training their new employees before sending them out on assignments. There are a lot of weaker guys that just give up before they get used to the fast pace of the job. Before you came to work here, it was just an endless cycle of people quitting."

"Is that right..."

"We're a small company, so the most we can usually do is hire some spoiled kids from a third-rate private university. But usually, their patience doesn't last for very long. Maybe it's because they didn't have to work hard to get into college, so they don't know what perseverance is. Or that could just be my own stereotype. But I'm sure the president has thought the exact same thing. When he received your phone call, he was really excited about you. He said someone like you, who had made it into an exclusive national university on the first try must have a lot of guts, and he wanted your talent for our company."

"So I guess that's why he came all the way from Tokyo to give me the interview. His enthusiasm persuaded me so much that before I knew it, I was here."

"I think you made the right decision. Weren't you originally going to find work back home? But instead, you changed your mind and came here for the first time. Thank you. Well, I guess it's kind of weird for me to thank you, but..." Hatanaka tried to hide his embarrassment by laughing loudly.

Katsuya felt a little guilty that Hatanaka had some kind of strange gratitude towards him. Honestly, Katsuya couldn't deny the fact that he had decided to work for the company because he had secretly hoped he would see Shio again, even though it seemed like those hopes were futile at this point.

According to Kazuki, Shio was simply an investor and was busy working with many other companies. He had looked at the company overview, and just as Kazuki had said, Shio was an executive of the company in name only. Katsuya hadn't heard any mention of him since he had first joined the company.

But he was the one who had told Kazuki not to

tell Shio anything, and in doing so, had destroyed his only chance of Shio knowing he was even there.

At this rate, he probably would *never* get to see Shio.

It was all about timing, after all.

Katsuya had first met Shio because of the perfect timing of just one summer; there was no guarantee that another coincidence like that would ever visit him again.

When he returned to the office, he recorded the day's lack of progress in the logbook and began to work on business proposals for the next day. Actually, since Katsuya was still inexperienced, he was just typing and copying proposals Hatanaka had already made.

"Everyone starts with making copies. Just remember this is part of the job, and concentrate," Hatanaka said as he unloaded a pile of manuscripts on Katsuya's desk. Katsuya looked up at him with a look of disbelief. Hatanaka returned his look with a grin and calmly walked away.

He had no choice, so he quickly finished typing and gathered up the pile of manuscripts.

He went to make copies at the copy machine near Human Resources and stared boredly at a row of nearby cabinets.

Suddenly, something caught his attention. Among the various files and items on the crowded shelves, there was a framed photograph in the corner.

It looked like it had been taken at the time the company was established. There were a lot fewer employees then; about eight men and women stood beside each other, smiling.

Among those faces was one Katsuya immediately recognized.

It was Shio-san. Katsuya took the picture in his hand and examined it closely. Shio was wearing a dark suit and looked very grown up. There was no doubt about it—Shio had the appearance of an outstanding member of society. And he definitely hadn't lost any of his unique appeal. He was beautiful.

It was difficult to explain exactly how, or in what way he was beautiful, but he possessed a certain refreshing beauty that normal men didn't have.

"What are you looking at?" a voice from behind asked, releasing Katsuya from his absorption with the picture.

As he turned, he saw Hiromi smiling. She peeked at the picture in Katsuya's hands.

"Oh, this picture here," he said.

"Ah, that's the picture that was taken when the company first began," Hiromi explained. "I wasn't working here at the time, but it seems the company was started with just those members. There's President Soga, Manager Tamano from Systems Development...Ahaha, Manager Miike has his eyes closed!"

"Do you know this person?" Katsuya pointed to Shio, and Hiromi's eyes began to sparkle.

"Yes, that's Executive Ozawa-san. Doesn't he look like he could be a model? Everyone says that because he's so slender and *totally* looks like Prince Charming. President said that Ozawa-san had a lot of agents try to scout him when he was a student...Ah, that's right, the president was one year ahead of Ozawa-san at university;

that's why they established the company together."

"Does he come here a lot?" Katsuya asked.

"No, now that you mention it, I haven't seen him at all lately. But he's involved with a lot of other companies, so I'm sure he's very busy."

"Is that so..." Katsuya was a bit disappointed. This reaffirmed his belief that he wouldn't get to see Shio after all. He gave one last lingering look at the picture he held in his hand, at Shio's smiling face.

This is probably the only way I'll ever see what Shio-san looks like now.

Before he saw the picture, he only remembered Shio's face as he had looked 12 years earlier, a junior high school student.

"Oh, that's right!" Hiromi suddenly exclaimed. "We're going to have a welcoming party for you, Narita-san. The president is super excited about it! All our co-workers will get together and celebrate. Right now, he's muttering to himself in his office, trying to figure out where we should have the party."

Katsuya looked up at Hiromi's face.

"The president is here right now?" he asked.

"Hmm? Yes, he just returned. He seems to be in a good mood and is reading magazines in his office."

There was something more important than a welcoming party right now; something much more important than deciding which restaurant they would go to—the company housing!

With nothing but a vague "Please wait a little longer," Katsuya's patience was wearing thin at the delay. Also, the hotel bills were piling up. He didn't even care if he couldn't stay at the company housing at this point. He could find a boarding house or an apartment by himself—all he wanted was to know exactly what was going on.

With an angry look on his face, Katsuya returned the picture to the shelf and made up his mind.

He was going to complain to the president directly.

He didn't like this unsettled feeling. He wasn't thinking about quitting the company, but he decided he would talk to the president himself if he had to.

"Na-Narita-san?" Hiromi stammered, and watched, dumbfounded, as Katsuya walked briskly towards the president's office.

The door was open.

The president always left the door open so people would feel free to come to him for advice at any time. Katsuya entered the room to find President Soga humming and looking through a magazine targeted towards young people.

He immediately noticed Katsuya and said, "Oh, Narita-kun! Great timing! I was thinking of having a welcoming party for you soon and was just looking for a good restaurant. How about this one? Or do you have a special request?"

"President!"

Soga looked up at him, startled by his loud exclamation. "You scared me, yelling out like that!"

"What is going on with the company housing?" Katsuya demanded, getting straight to the point.

Soga looked as if he just remembered something

and murmured, "Ah..."

A guilty look spread across his face, as if he realized he had finally been caught.

Katsuya pressed on. "President, you said not to worry about where I should live when I came to Tokyo. That you'd have proper company housing ready for me, and that you'd completely support my move. I trusted you, and that's why I came here. Naturally, I thought I'd be finished moving in before I started work, but you haven't made any arrangements at all for me! If that's all it is, then I can't do anything. But since you keep telling me to wait, I want to know what's going on with the company housing, and when I can move in. Don't you think I'm entitled to that at least?"

"Ah...y-yes, you're right..." Soga mumbled as Katsuya approached him.

Katsuya, who seemed like a quiet person, could be forceful when it really mattered.

"I'm living in a hotel that I'm not used to, and even when I sleep through the whole night, I still wake up exhausted. I have to have a place of my own or I just can't relax or feel any relief. If the company housing isn't possible, then just tell me. I won't even care if you tell me the company housing was a mistake on your part, and that I should find an apartment. But what I can't stand is not knowing whether it is available or not. Should I look for an apartment myself or just bear with staying in a hotel for now? I just want to know what to do!"

Suddenly, Soga slapped both hands on top of his desk with a loud bang, and bent himself forward. "I...I'm sorry. I didn't realize this had become such a big burden for you. I'm very sorry," he apologized earnestly.

But Katsuya wasn't seeking an apology. All he wanted was just one thing—a solution to his problem.

"It would have been different if I knew I had to stay in a hotel until a certain date, but being in a situation where I'm not told anything except to wait is just too much," he said.

"I'm sorry..." Soga repeated.

"So I guess the story about the company housing..." *Was a lie.* Katsuya finished the sentence in his head. *But why would he tell a lie that would be found out so easily? Maybe the plans for the company housing just hadn't advanced as quickly as he had hoped.*

Soga looked flustered and said, "No, no...actually, the date was pushed back, and I wasn't sure what to do about it myself. But it's fine now! I have somewhere for you to live."

"Really? Are you serious?" Katsuya blinked in disbelief at this sudden development.

"Yes. I had been thinking about it before, but that doesn't get anything accomplished. It's a condo in Higashinakano. It's pretty spacious, more like a dormitory than a condo."

"A...dormitory?"

"Company housing" had now turned into "company dormitory."

However, at this point, anything was better than staying in a hotel. Whether it was a dorm or company housing, Katsuya couldn't complain. All he wanted was his own place where he could relax; a place where he could be alone and at ease.

"Yes, but actually, you'd have a roommate. There's already someone living there. You're about the same age, so I'm sure you'll get along fine. I'll give him a call right away, so can you wait a bit?" Soga said, and began dialing the phone on his desk.

Once again, he had been told to wait. Katsuya returned to the tedious task of making copies, still full of doubts.

Before a half-hour had passed the main office door opened. Katsuya was still busy with work so he didn't see the person who headed straight for the president's office. After a while, Hiromi came over to him.

"Narita-san, the president would like to see you," she said.

"Ah, thanks," Katsuya said.

However, Hiromi didn't return to her desk after passing the message along, but instead started to gather up the stack of finished copies. Standing beside Katsuya, she softly whispered, "The man we were just talking about, Ozawa-san..."

"What about him?"

"He just went to see the president, for the first time in a while. And since he wants to see you, this is probably about the company housing situation."

Hearing that Shio was there, Katsuya swallowed hard. However, he didn't see what this had to do with the company housing situation.

"What do you mean?" he asked.

"I don't know, ask him yourself. Also, just so you know, the whole office had heard what you said to the president earlier." Hiromi flashed him a mischievous smile and then returned to her desk.

Katsuya stood frozen for a while, but he knew he couldn't make Shio and the president wait much longer. He hurriedly straightened up the copied manuscripts and headed towards Soga's office.

The door was closed. He knocked lightly, nervously saying, "It's Narita," and slowly opened the door.

Shio was in the room. He turned towards the doorway and stared silently at Katsuya. Soga was sitting at his desk, and invited Katsuya inside with a broad smile on his face.

Katsuya entered the room hesitantly, and stood next to Shio. He suddenly realized that even though he used to be much shorter than Shio, he was now slightly taller than him.

However, Shio was still as slender as ever, and had a clever beauty about him that hadn't been captured in the photograph.

Soga began to speak. "Ah, Narita-kun. This is Shio Ozawa, a founding member and executive of the company. And this is Katsuya Narita, a new employee whom we have high hopes for this year. Ozawa's housing is provided for by the company. A lot has happened, but starting today, it will now be a company dormitory. And Narita-kun will be living there. It's already furnished, so you can move in right away without any special preparations. I hope you find your dormitory life enjoyable."

Shio said nothing.

When Katsuya entered the room, Shio had

glanced at him, but now he faced the president, silent and expressionless.

"Oh, that's right. Narita-kun, just because Ozawa is an executive, please don't feel uncomfortable. At home, company titles don't matter at all! As a rule of this dormitory, you two must get along and treat each other as equals. Anyway, you're close to the same age, so I'm sure you'll get along just fine."

"Yes..." Katsuya mumbled.

Katsuya had little confidence that that would be the case. After all, he had just resigned himself to the idea that he'd never see Shio again, and suddenly, they had become roommates! He couldn't just say, "Oh, okay!" and accept it so easily.

He wondered what Shio thought of all this, and stole a glance at the other man's face.

Shio was still looking silently at Soga. Even though he had just had a huge load of luggage named Katsuya forced upon him, there was no change in his calm expression.

Soga continued, "Well then, it's decided. Ozawa will take you to get your things from the hotel, and then you may go home. He brought his car, so the timing is perfect. Oh, and tell HR tomorrow that you've found a new place to live. They said you wrote down the hotel's address as your own! Well, you just can't do that..."

But Hiromi-san had said that I could, and she works in HR....

Well, anyway, the most important thing right now was whether or not Shio himself agreed to this arrangement or not.

Just as Katsuya was about to ask Shio, Soga beat him to the punch. "Hey, Ozawa. Don't just stand there. And Narita-kun, you too. You look like a scared, abandoned puppy! Okay? Everyone is okay with this, right?" he said weakly.

Katsuya, the abandoned puppy, also wanted to hear the answer, and cleared his throat nervously.

"Okay with it?" Shio's clear voice rang in Katsuya's ears. "No, I'm *not* okay with it. Our original agreement was that I would live alone. But now, all of a sudden, I have to have a roommate? That's unbelievable. I understand you're in a different situation here, Soga-san, and I understand that leaving this problem unsolved would create problems for the company. I suppose I have no choice."

"Oh, great! Thanks, Ozawa!" Soga stood and extended his hand out to Shio.

Shio ignored him and continued, "You don't have to thank me. But there's one thing I want to make perfectly clear." His clear voice reverberated in the president's office. "I do not need a roommate. The only reason I'm doing this is because you're basically forcing me to, and I certainly don't need a roommate who is my "equal," as you said. Is that clear? However, I will compromise and let him stay with me as long as he understands that he is completely on his own."

Chapter 3

After that, Shio took Katsuya to the hotel so he could check out. Then they headed towards his condo in Higashinakano. Inside the car, the two men were completely silent. Or rather, they wanted to talk, but couldn't find the words. Loaded up with one overnight bag and a freeloader, Shio's car sped through the city at night. Ever since they had left the office, Katsuya had been wondering if Shio really thought of him as a troublesome burden. However, Shio did not make any effort to talk to him, or even glance at him; he just kept driving silently. Since he was obviously being rejected, Katsuya didn't dare to try speaking to Shio himself.

Instead, Katsuya began to feel regret. Just as the president had said, he was about to begin his dormitory life living as a freeloader in Shio's condo. His head spun at this sudden development, and he felt as if he hadn't been able to make a level-headed decision. He couldn't imagine how much trouble he was causing Shio by moving in with him. But honestly, up until the point they had left the office, happiness had won out. The joy of having finally seen Shio, whom he had been longing to see all this time. The sense of relief that he would now have his own place to relax, even though it was a dorm.

However, that happiness had quickly faded. Now, Katsuya's heart was troubled by the disappointed feeling that he would be causing trouble for others. Shio, the person he had longed for all this time, was right beside him, yet he seemed so far away.

Shio's hands gripped the steering wheel, and he stared straight ahead, not even once looking at Katsuya. Seeing Shio's cold profile, Katsuya suddenly felt like running away.

At last, they turned off the main road into a residential area. Katsuya stared out the window at the rows of houses, wondering if they were almost home yet, when the car turned left into an underground parking lot beneath a condo complex. It seemed like they had reached their destination.

Shio quickly got out of the car and looked at Katsuya. Flustered, Katsuya grabbed his overnight bag and also got out of the car.

"Seventh floor, number 713," Shio said, talking to Katsuya for the first time.

Even though it was just Shio brusquely telling him the room number, Katsuya felt a little relieved.

They took the elevator from the parking lot to the seventh floor. Shio stepped out into the hallway first, followed by Katsuya. He unlocked a door at the end of the hallway.

"This is it."

At Shio's prompting, Katsuya entered the room hesitantly.

On the left side of the foyer was a door that led to the bathroom. Straight down the hall was a wooden door with a glass window. The hallway continued to the right. Following Shio through the door, they entered a large open room containing the kitchen, living room and dining room. The room was mainly decorated in beige, and a large LCD television sat on top of an elegant credenza. The room contained only the bare necessities; it was as neat as a pin.

Still clutching his bag, Katsuya looked around the room restlessly.

Shio spoke. "There are three rooms. One is my bedroom, one is the office, and the last one is a room I've been using as a storage room. You can use that one. There's a closet in there, so you can put away your things. I'm sure you'll have plenty of space."

"Okay, thank you very much."

"You don't have to worry about the rent or utilities. As long as you pay for your own personal items and food, you can use anything you like. I only have one rule if you're going to live here: mind your own business. That's it."

"Um..." Katsuya said hesitantly.

"What?" Shio asked with a sudden, surprisingly kind look on his face. Even though it flashed on his face for only a moment, it was more than enough to make Katsuya's heart pound.

"Should we take turns making meals?" he asked.

Shio was silent.

Katsuya continued, "I think it would be a lot more economical if we took turns cooking, and ate together instead of separately. If it's okay with you, I'd be more than happy to..."

"Like I said, you don't have to bother," Shio said. "I usually eat out, anyway. Just because I have a roommate now doesn't mean I'm going to change my lifestyle. Don't waste your time."

"But..." Katsuya wanted to say, "But there's no way you eat out for all three meals, right?", but he thought it might be considered as not minding his own business, so he closed his mouth. Shio would probably be annoyed at any further attempts to be persuaded to take turns making food. After all, Katsuya's presence was nothing but a burden to him.

"Shio-san..."

Katsuya had wanted to apologize, but that slipped out instead. Even though he should have called him "Ozawa-san" in this situation, he had called him by the name he had always called him inside of his heart. Even if Shio recognized Katsuya, he hadn't made any mention of it yet.

Shio just looked at Katsuya after his name had been called. As he locked eyes with Shio, Katsuya felt as if time had stopped in that moment.

Shio slowly took off his coat and threw it over the back of the sofa. With a sigh, he sat down. "Have you already seen Kazuki?"

"What? Um...yes!" Katsuya said, surprised. Since Shio had suddenly brought up Kazuki, that must mean he remembered Katsuya. "Shio-san, do you remember me?" he asked eagerly.

That fateful summer 12 years ago...he couldn't believe that Shio would actually remember him. Katsuya's heart suddenly swelled.

"Until I saw you, I thought it was just someone who had the same name as you. Kazuki had told me that you had found work back in your hometown. So when Soga-san called me and talked to me about getting a roommate, I never imagined it would be you." Shio's cool reaction to their reunion was in direct contrast with Katsuya's emotions.

"I'm sorry...I did get a job there, but a lot happened, so I decided to come work here," Katsuya explained.

"Okay, then," Shio said.

"I saw Kazuki already. He was the one who found me the hotel I was staying at."

Shio frowned. "What was he thinking? He should have found you a reasonable apartment instead of a hotel room!"

"No, I'm the one who asked him to," Katsuya protested. "He just helped me out with my request."

Shio still seemed dissatisfied. It was no wonder; he was suddenly forced to have a roommate in his elegant condo. It's not like he was going to welcome Katsuya with open arms.

Flustered, Katsuya changed the subject. "But Shio-san, you didn't act like you knew me at all in front of the president, so I totally thought you didn't remember who I was."

"If I had acted like I knew you that would have been playing right into Soga-san's plan. He would have said, 'Oh, well if you're already acquaintances, what's the problem?' I would have had no way to protest. I didn't want any part of that underhanded stuff."

"Underhanded?"

"He would have acted like since I know you, I should automatically want to help you. I don't like that kind of attitude. Bringing up something that happened when I was a kid would be the worst. So if I absolutely have to, I'd rather live with a complete stranger."

That's pretty cold. Definitely not a reaction someone would have after seeing me for the first time in 12 years. To Shio, Katsuya was just someone he merely recognized, and he probably wouldn't care if Katsuya was dying by the roadside.

Katsuya felt hollow and his shoulders dropped in disappointment. What had he been hoping for anyway? They were never that close to begin with, so it wasn't like Shio would be thrilled at seeing him again, anyway. He was definitely friends with Kazuki. But what about Shio? There was nothing between them. To Shio, he was merely a familiar face, a friend of his brother's.

That night, Katsuya found it hard to fall asleep on his simple mattress that was spread on the floor. Shio was in the same house. But he knew Shio found his presence to be unpleasant, which made being in the same house as Shio even more painful. Being away from Shio was lonely, but being close to the other man and not being able to express his feelings only made his loneliness grow. Katsuya learned that for the first time that night.

* * *

The next morning, Katsuya woke up early and began to make coffee in the kitchen. He wanted to make breakfast, but there were neither eggs nor bread, so coffee would have to suffice. As Shio had said, it looked like it was rare for him to cook for himself at home. It seemed like the only thing he used the kitchen for was to make coffee and tea.

As Katsuya sipped his coffee, he made a shopping list of food and supplies he would need. The glass door opened, and Shio appeared, wearing a suit. He looked like he was all ready for work: he wore a necktie and a white dress shirt, he had his coat thrown over his arm, and his other hand held a leather briefcase.

In the morning light, Shio seemed so beautiful and fresh. It was almost blinding, and Katsuya narrowed his eyes instinctively.

As he noticed the mellow aroma that filled the room, Shio looked at Katsuya.

"Good morning. I made some coffee. Would you like some?" Katsuya asked cheerfully. He took out another cup and was about to pour some coffee into it when Shio waved his hand at him.

"No, don't bother." Shio coldly refused.

Katsuya obeyed as Shio went on.

"I usually come home quite late, so as I said yesterday, just eat without me. As long as you don't go into my room, you can use whatever you like. Oh, and here's the key. Try not to lose it."

"Okay." Katsuya picked up the key Shio had tossed onto the table.

"See you later." After saying everything he wanted to, Shio left. The sound of the front door slamming sounded hollow.

Katsuya had no idea where Shio was going. For that matter, he had no idea what Shio's job consisted of at all. He was miserable because in their current situation, he wouldn't even be allowed to ask Shio such questions.

When he got to work, Hatanaka pounded him on the shoulder. "Hey, so you finally got that company housing! Good for you!" It seemed news of him moving had spread.

"Well, it's more like a dorm than company housing."

"Well, they're basically the same, aren't they? You said you wanted to get settled as soon as possible, didn't you?"

"Yes, that's right." Katsuya gave Hatanaka a forced smile and sighed quietly. Company housing and a dorm only *seemed* similar. It was true that he had wanted to settle down quickly, but he didn't feel that was possible if he had to live with Shio.

In any case, Kazuki had helped him out, so he thought he should give him a call. He called Kazuki on his cell phone and told him he had moved to a company dorm. Kazuki was so happy one would almost think it was happening to him. Katsuya wanted to talk to him about Shio, but decided not to do it over the phone.

"Do you want to meet up tonight?" he asked.

"Sure," Kazuki replied.

He decided to be completely honest with Kazuki and ask for his friend's advice. Since Kazuki knew both him and Shio well, Katsuya felt that his friend would have some good ideas about what to do in this situation.

After arranging the night's meeting, Katsuya returned to his desk to find Hatanaka waiting for him, already prepared to leave.

"What are you doing? We gotta get going!" Hatanaka barked. Katsuya quickly grabbed his briefcase and followed his senior out the door.

* * *

That night, Kazuki met Katsuya at the Shinjuku station, and brought him to a favorite bar of his. There were both small and large tables lined up inside the large bar. There were already a few customers enjoying their food and drinks when they got there. Inside the place, the smell of alcohol mixed with the scent of tobacco.

They made their way through the lively bar, and were shown to a small corner table. Settling down, Kazuki raised his hand and ordered beer and some food.

"Well, let's celebrate you getting company housing!" he said gleefully.

"Celebrate?" Katsuya asked.

"You don't look very happy. You finally got the company housing you've been waiting for! Cheer up!" Kazuki raised his mug of beer.

Katsuya smiled and raised his glass. "Cheers!" Their glasses clinked together in a toast.

He hadn't had beer for quite a while, and the taste of it bit at his throat. But a cold beer after work was definitely refreshing. He was exhausted after making the rounds of their regular clients again that day with Hatanaka. Hatanaka had laughed and told him that that was how work was supposed to make him feel. Even if clients refused their offers, if he kept going back, they would start to remember his face. Pretty soon, he would be able to make more conversations with the clients. Hatanaka had told him perseverance was necessary in order to sell a new person's name and face. Katsuya felt like he was just beginning to sense how important his job was.

"Well, where *is* the company housing?" Kazuki asked as he took a bite of food.

"Higashinakano," Katsuya answered. "It's about eight minutes from the train station by foot."

"Wow, so is it an apartment or a condo?"

"It's a condo."

"That's so weird! My brother lives in a condo in Higashinakano! I wonder if you're in the same neighborhood."

Katsuya hesitated. "Um, actually..."

"What?"

Just as he thought, Katsuya figured it would be hard for Kazuki to even imagine him living with Shio. *He's in for another surprise,* he thought, and started to explain.

"Actually, the condo in Higashinakano...is less like company housing and more like a dormitory situation."

"A dorm?"

"Yeah. Apparently, the plans the president had for my company housing fell through. But since he had promised me, he made me move in with someone who was already living alone in company housing."

"Wow, that sounds terrible."

"Yeah, that's what I thought, too. But who cares about me; I feel terrible for the guy who was forced to take me in! They changed the terms of his company housing and everything."

"Well, yeah, if they told him he'd be living alone in the beginning, I'd feel bad for him, too."

"So that's why I'm not completely happy, even though I found a place to live. All I'm doing is causing trouble for him," Katsuya said in a depressed tone.

Kazuki interrupted him quickly, "Now, don't be so negative! Maybe he's happy that he made a new friend?"

"I don't know..." Katsuya tilted his head. After the way Shio had acted yesterday and today, he highly doubted that.

"So how old is your roommate?"

"About 26."

"He's close to our age! It's not like you're from a different generation or something, so maybe you'll actually hit it off? He might be like an older brother to you."

"It's Shio-san," Katsuya finally said.

"What?"

"My roommate is Shio-san."

Kazuki's eyes grew wide in surprise, just like a cartoon character. "What? What? WHAT?" he exclaimed loudly. People from other tables looked over in annoyance, but Kazuki was oblivious to it. He was at a loss for words. Suddenly, he snapped back to reality, drained his beer mug, ordered another from a waiter passing by, and turned to Katsuya. "You mean...Shio, my *brother*, Shio?"

"Yes."

"Whaaaat?" another yell of amazement came from Kazuki's mouth, although this one was a bit quieter. His refill of beer came, and he gulped it down quickly and sighed. "I'm shocked."

"Looks like it."

"I'm just...surprised."

"I was, too, when the president called me in and Shio-san was standing there. I was surprised just to see his face, but then the president told me I'd be moving in with him!"

"Yeah, I guess so. I can't believe Shio agreed to it," Kazuki said in disbelief.

"He really didn't agree to it. He was forced to. I think he couldn't say no to the president. Even I know that must have put Shio-san in a difficult position," Katsuya murmured with self-derision. He gulped down his beer.

Kazuki looked at Katsuya worriedly. "Well, I'm sure Shio's annoyed that his solitary lifestyle was changed, but on the other hand, isn't this a good story for you? It's better than having to move in with a complete stranger. Shio probably agreed to the living arrangement because he's known you for so long."

If Katsuya said he wasn't happy that he was living with Shio, he would be lying. But on the other hand, if Shio would have readily taken him in, no matter how happy he would be, he would still be sorry for causing trouble. As Katsuya hung his head silently, Kazuki reached his hand out to his friend. Feeling a hand on his face, Katsuya looked up to see Kazuki looking back at him with a troubled expression. "Don't look so sad!"

"When I think that I'm making Shio-san unhappy, it's hard for me, too..." Katsuya whispered.

"Now, stop over-exaggerating!"

"I'm not."

"What do you mean?"

"The real reason I came to Tokyo...is because of Shio-san."

Kazuki held his breath; he was surprised for the second time that night.

"I didn't make it clear to you the other day at the hotel, but I joined the company because of Shio-san, too. Because I wanted to see him."

"Katsuya..."

"But it's wrong to get a job because of that kind of ulterior motive, isn't it? When you told me Shio-san works for other companies, I realized that I couldn't always get my way. I had no idea what I'd do when I see him, anyway. But...I just hoped that I'd have even the slightest chance of seeing him."

Kazuki was silent.

"So I had a change of heart, and just when I was about to forget about him and put all my efforts into work, I found out I'd be living with him. I never could have imagined this would happen."

He was mainly complaining, but Kazuki listened to him quietly. Katsuya put all the bad feelings he'd held inside into words and told Kazuki about them, and he felt his heart get a little lighter.

When he was finished speaking, Kazuki had his arms crossed across his chest and looked like he was deep in thought. Katsuya rested his chin on his hands silently.

It seemed like they weren't even in a lively bar, and both sat quietly together.

"Two more beers, please!" Kazuki suddenly said, stopping a busy waiter that was passing by the table. Then, he turned towards Katsuya and said, "Do you like my brother?" As usual, he got straight to the point.

"If you asked me if I like him or hate him, I'd say that I like him. But what you're actually asking me is if I have any kind of romantic feelings for him, aren't you?" It was easier for Katsuya to answer that way rather than avoiding the issue.

"Yeah."

"I'm not even sure of the answer to that. Sometimes I think I do, but then sometimes, I think I just admire him."

"For how long?"

"Ever since you two came to visit that summer."

Actually, Katsuya was troubled by the fact that he wasn't sure of his feelings. He wasn't sure what he should do next, or how he should behave. He wondered if he should just stay quietly in the background so he didn't upset Shio any further. Or maybe he should just give up and look for his own apartment. He had very few options, and pondered what he should do next. He didn't think any of them were good ideas, but couldn't think of any other possibilities. What he was certain of was he didn't want to cause trouble for Shio.

"I don't think my brother has any feelings for you," Kazuki said bluntly, interrupting Katsuya's thoughts.

"I know that." Katsuya said.

"I don't mean that he hates you or anything," Kazuki clarified quickly. "But, it's...he barely knows you. He never had the chance to get to know you. From his perspective, you're pretty much a stranger to him. And not just that, but Shio's only ever dated girls."

"I know," Katsuya repeated.

"He's always been really popular with the ladies, to the point where he's never been turned down. He had a girlfriend in college that he was really considering a future with."

Well, Shio was handsome and intelligent, so that didn't surprise Katsuya. He was happy to hear that Shio had always been loved by many people.

"That's Shio-san for you," he said.

"Apparently, they broke up after graduation," Kazuki continued explaining. "After that, Shio kind of changed. As if, he didn't trust people much anymore. Or maybe it's better to say that he didn't believe in love anymore. So since then, he hasn't had another serious relationship; he's just been messing around."

"Did she cheat on him?" Katsuya asked.

"That's what I think happened. Shio doesn't talk to me about that kind of stuff, so I don't know for sure, though."

"I see..."

"So it doesn't really matter what you do. I think it's a problem with him. So even if you have feelings for him, it doesn't matter."

Katsuya knew Kazuki was just saying these things because his friend was worried about him. He also knew that falling in love with someone who didn't love him back would only hurt him in the end. Maybe that's what Kazuki was trying to say.

"I know that," Katsuya sighed. "I never really considered that something could happen between us. I think that if I did, I would have come to Tokyo a lot earlier."

"So you just admire Shio?"

"Maybe. When I was a child, Shio-san was the first person I'd met that had that kind of refined, city image. It really stuck with me. I've always idolized Shio-san as someone who is beautiful both inside and out."

"Who cares about his looks...he has a pretty severe personality, you know," Kazuki said, and Katsuya smiled understandingly.

"Yeah, I kind of noticed. Shio-san is probably a lot stricter than I could ever imagine, but that's probably just how he is. So you shouldn't worry, Kazuki. I'm busy enough trying to learn my new job, so I don't have time to worry about other things. I've finally been given a place where I can relax. I'll try not to think about unnecessary things and just do my best at work."

"Katsuya." Kazuki had a relieved look on his face.

Katsuya really surprised Kazuki by suddenly telling his friend that Shio was the reason he came to Tokyo. On top of that, Kazuki probably found it hard to relate to a man being obsessed with another man. Of course, it was even harder for Katsuya himself to understand it. Those strange, exhilarating feelings of the summer 12 years earlier...those feelings he couldn't forget...that he had closed away deep in his heart. He still wondered exactly what those feelings were.

He said goodbye to Kazuki a little after 10:00 p.m. and headed home. He got off the train at Higashinakano station and hurried towards the condo, when he suddenly remembered the shopping list he had made that morning. It was already late at night. The shops near the train station were already closed. The only thing open at this time would be the 24-hour convenience store.

He decided he'd just buy the things he absolutely needed, and dropped by the convenience store. He bought some bread, eggs and milk for the next day. He also bought some changes of underclothes, and then headed towards the condo.

When he arrived home, it was already 11:00 p.m., and the place was dark; it looked like Shio wasn't home yet. As he placed the groceries in the fridge, he thought about what he should do the next day. Should he do as Shio said and not interfere with his roommate? Should he just worry about himself in this strange lifestyle, or should he just say to hell with it and interact with Shio however he wanted to, even though he knew it would annoy the other man?

He made some coffee to sober himself up. As he sipped it, he rested his chin on his hand and lost himself in thought. Kazuki had said so, but he still thought it would be unnatural to act like Shio wasn't even there. Of course he didn't have any kind of strange ulterior motives; he just wanted to get along with him as a roommate.

But would even having those feelings bother Shio? As Katsuya put down his cup, he looked around the silent living room.

A large, beautiful condo. Yet the two people who lived in it didn't even talk to each other or eat together. He didn't want their relationship to be like that.

Katsuya made a decision. No matter what Shio said, he'd just think of this situation as good luck on his part. Even though he felt distant from Shio, being together with the person he admired made him happy. That's what their connection meant to him. Whatever happens will happen. So he decided to stop thinking that he was a nuisance to Shio.

One of Katsuya's merits was that he was positive and cheerful. He was satisfied with that.

That night, Katsuya slept soundly on his hard mattress. It was the first time that he had had a truly deep sleep since he had come to Tokyo.

Chapter 4

Starting the next day, Katsuya began to wake up early in the morning and made breakfast. He usually made something simple like toast and milk with a salad or ham and egg. He placed both his and Shio's portions on the table. Shio awakened to Katsuya cheerfully preparing breakfast, and stared at the plates on the table with an annoyed look on his face.

"I thought I told you not to bother with stuff like this," he said, just as Katsuya had expected him to.

"It's pretty delicious. You should try some," Katsuya offered, smiling.

Shio shook his head with a disgusted look on his face, and went back to the living room. Katsuya waited a bit before he went ahead and ate. When he was finished, Shio still hadn't come back to the table. He hadn't been expecting him to, anyway, so he didn't let it bother him. He decided to pack Shio's uneaten portion in a plastic container and eat it for lunch. While he was quickly wrapping up his lunch, he heard Shio's footsteps going toward the entryway and hurriedly followed him.

"Let's go to the train station together," he said. Shio looked at him in surprise. Katsuya returned his look with a smile, but Shio began to walk away nonetheless, as if to say, "No way." However, Katsuya didn't let it bother him and followed Shio to the train station anyway.

He continued to go to work in this fashion every morning, and stopped at the supermarket every day after work to pick up groceries for dinner. Since Katsuya's parents both worked, he was a fairly good cook. He had been in charge of cooking at club training camps during high school and college, so he knew how to cook most of the usual things.

He prepared a healthy, balanced dinner, and then waited until 9:00 p.m. for Shio to come home. If it seemed like Shio would be later than that, he would go ahead and eat without him, saving Shio's portion so he could heat it up later.

When Shio returned home, Katsuya would tell him that he made dinner. Every time, Shio made an annoyed face, but Katsuya still offered him the food cheerfully. Usually, Shio would say that he had already eaten, but occasionally, he would give in and eat the food Katsuya had put so much effort into.

"Don't you have things to do?" Shio once asked. "There's no reason for you to make breakfast and dinner, and wait around every day. I told you before, we're only roommates. You don't need to bother with this."

"It's not a bother at all," Katsuya insisted. "I'm used to making meals. I enjoy it, actually. If I'm going to make dinner anyway, making one more portion isn't a big deal. It's more fun to eat with someone else rather than eating alone, anyway."

"...Fun?"

Even though Shio often acted annoyed, Katsuya truly believed that there wasn't anyone who would be upset after being offered delicious food. However,

Katsuya made sure not to bother Shio any further. He figured it was just in Shio's nature to avoid interacting with people he wasn't familiar with.

No matter what kind of living arrangement you had, rules were necessary. Katsuya intended to respect what Shio had said. While respecting each other's rules, they both tried to compromise and play things by ear as well. The effect of that showed itself more quickly than expected.

It was Saturday, his day off from work. Katsuya woke up around the usual time, and started his first task of the day—making breakfast. He usually just made toast and milk, but yesterday, he had thought it would be nice to have rice and miso soup every once in a while, so on the way home from work he had picked up some ingredients. Katsuya had always loved Japanese food. If he could have it his way, he would eat rice and miso soup every morning, but that would be very time consuming.

He couldn't spare even one more minute, one more second of his busy mornings, so he had made only toast for breakfast. But since he was off that day, he was happy that he could spend as much time cooking as he liked. He made some spinach seasoned with soy sauce and some grilled fish. Next, he expertly fried an egg, and then began to make the miso soup, using some kelp for stock. The main ingredients for his miso soup were simply onions and seaweed. To that, he added a bunch of toasted sesame seeds. That was Katsuya's own style of making miso soup.

After the rice had finished cooking, Katsuya wondered what he should do next. Since he had gone to all the trouble of making such an elaborate Japanese meal, he wanted to share it with Shio, but he also didn't want to put his roommate in one of his moods by waking him up early on a weekend. Shio had come home especially late the night before, so Katsuya wanted to let him rest. As he began to eat by himself, the living room door quietly opened.

Startled, Katsuya looked up to see Shio come into the room unsteadily. He was wearing pajamas and looked like he was still half-asleep. He plodded towards Katsuya on his bare feet with the pleasant *pitter-patter* sound a sleepy child would make.

"Ah...good morning," Katsuya said.

Without answering Katsuya, Shio tilted his head as if it were very heavy, and rested it in his right hand.

"Um, I made breakfast, would you like some?"

Shio didn't answer.

"I tried making a Japanese breakfast this morning," Katsuya babbled. "It's only grilled fish, a seasoned dish, a fried egg...but if you'd like some, go ahead."

However, Shio absentmindedly looked around the kitchen as if he hadn't heard a word Katsuya had said.

As his gaze fell on the table, he shuffled over and sniffed loudly.

"Smells good..." he murmured.

Huh? Katsuya thought. *Did the smell of my cooking wake him up and lead him all the way here?* That was amazing in and of itself, but Katsuya wondered which smell exactly had such an effect on Shio and sniffed the air himself.

The smell of hot rice, the savory smell of the grilled fish, the sweet smell of the fried egg...but out of all of the various smells, the smell of the miso soup definitely stood out the most. Just then, Shio pointed at the miso soup and said, "Do I smell sesame?"

Katsuya began to feel happy as he realized it had been the smell of the miso soup that Shio was reacting to. "Yes, I like putting toasted sesame seeds in my miso soup."

"It smells so good...so nostalgic," Shio said, captivated.

"Did your family add sesame seeds to your miso soup, too?"

"A long time ago, when I went to my uncle's house...he made miso soup that smelled like this. I loved the taste of it so much, but my mom couldn't make it like my uncle did. It's been such a long time..."

His uncle's house? He must be talking about that summer 12 years ago, when he came to the country, Katsuya thought. He was just modeling his miso soup after his own mother's recipe. But maybe adding toasted sesame seeds to miso soup was a regional thing.

"Shio-san, go ahead and eat. It should be pretty good, so I think you'll like it."

"No, it's okay." Even though he had sniffed so eagerly, Shio turned away from the offer in a huff.

"What? Why?"

"I told you not to bother."

"But don't you want to eat some? I made some for you, too. Don't be so stubborn."

"I'm not being stubborn. But on the condition that

you're living here for free, you're not supposed to bother yourself with this kind of thing. I've told you over and over again."

Apparently, Shio was wide awake now and back to his old self.

"But you ate the dinner I made for you the other day!" Once, Shio had come home in the middle of the night and had eaten the dinner Katsuya had saved for him. Shio pouted as Katsuya pointed this out to him.

"That's only because I was starving."

"Starving?"

"Also, it would have been a waste to throw away food." Shio was insincere as always.

At any rate, Katsuya never threw away any of the food; if it was still uneaten, he just ate it the next day. Still, Shio remained spiteful. Why couldn't he just admit that he had eaten it because he was hungry and he wanted to?

"Shio-san, you're contradicting yourself. Was it because you were starving or because you didn't want to waste the food? Pick one!"

"Okay, I was starving, then," Shio calmly answered.

He was acting so much like a child that it was adorable, and Katsuya suppressed a chuckle. If prideful Shio was laughed at by Katsuya, there was no way he'd show his true feelings around him anymore.

"Okay, then. Let's just say you're starving now, too. Come on, let's eat while it's warm. We finally have some rice. It would be wasteful if it got cold." Maybe he was reacting to the word "wasteful," but Shio hesitantly sat down at the table.

Relieved, Katsuya served Shio his food, placing the dishes in front of him. Facing each other at the table, they both began to eat quietly. Katsuya watched him, trying to see if he liked it or not. At first, Shio looked like he wasn't in the mood, but he quickly showed a hearty appetite. He obviously enjoyed the miso soup, as he quickly ate it. Katsuya figured he probably wouldn't ask for seconds, so he quietly refilled his bowl for him.

"Thanks..." Shio murmured, without looking up. Katsuya smiled. Maybe because he was so handsome and unapproachable, or maybe it was how he had so coldly protested when they first moved in together, but there was a time when Katsuya seriously thought Shio might be a cold-hearted person. But seeing him sitting there, eating like this, he just looked like a regular hungry guy.

"Do you like it?"

"Yeah, it's delicious," Shio answered, nodding earnestly.

"I'm glad. I'm pretty confident about my cooking."

"Confident?"

"Yeah. Maybe it's because my parents both worked ever since I was little. I had a lot of opportunities to help prepare meals. But I really model my recipes after my mom's cooking. This miso soup tastes just like my mom's too."

"Your mother's cooking?" Shio murmured.

That's right. Shio had mentioned that the smell of Katsuya's miso soup was nostalgic. The Shio that

Katsuya knew was only the boy that stayed at his uncle's house in the country 12 years ago, and the businessman that worked with many different companies. Now that he thought about it, Kazuki had never talked about their parents much. He wasn't sure if their mother had cooked for them much or not. However, Shio had called Katsuya's mother's cooking delicious right in front of him; he couldn't be happier.

Soon after, they finished eating. Shio curtly said, "Thank you for the food," and stood up. He was about to leave the room when he looked as if he had just remembered something, and began to clear the dishes from the table.

"Oh, I'll do it," Katsuya said, but Shio ignored him and set the dishes in the sink. He picked up a sponge and began scrubbing and washing the dishes.

So, he might be a good person after all, Katsuya thought with a smile as he watched him wash both of their dishes.

Shio ended up doing all the work, so Katsuya quietly thanked him. Shio waved him off with a bit of an embarrassed look on his face, and went into the living room. After he was out of earshot, Katsuya let out the breath he had been holding in. The shy expression on Shio's face was so refreshing and pretty.

* * *

Shio Ozawa had always enjoyed living alone. He lived in a beautiful condo and enjoyed spending time there by himself, not bothered by other people. When he was busy with work, all he wanted to do was return to his castle so he could relax, without having to worry about anything. Away from all of his obligations, a place where he could rest and take it easy. Since he was always so busy with work, that free time was his only source of happiness.

And then, he was suddenly forced to share it with someone else.

He had firmly turned him down, but President Soga had done a lot for him. He had gotten down on his hands and knees and begged him—Shio just couldn't say no after that. So he had had no choice but to take in a young man named Katsuya Narita. Even though he had laid the ground rules at first, Shio soon felt himself falling into Katsuya's pace.

Every morning, he woke up to a warm breakfast, and there was always dinner waiting for him when he came home from work. Katsuya kept the living room, dining room and bathroom spotless. It was actually cleaner than when Shio had lived there by himself.

Also, the smell of the coffee Katsuya made, the smell of his miso soup, stirred up something inside of him. He was grateful for it because it made him realize over and over again how hungry he had been for a regular, decent meal.

He thought Katsuya was a strange man. He was tall and tan, with an athletic build. He probably played sports. He had a clean-cut face. His honest eyes portrayed his serious personality perfectly.

He had heard from Soga that Katsuya was a rare find nowadays—an honest, innocent man. He had recently graduated from college, and Soga said he had wanted to hire him for his sincerity. Shio figured Soga had spent a lot of money trying to get Katsuya to work for him.

It was understandable. Shio had started to get to know Katsuya's good personality and even temperament, even though they had only lived together for about 10 days.

One day, Shio was very busy in the morning, but managed to wrap up his work by late afternoon. He had a reservation for dinner with a client that evening, and was on his way to the restaurant when he suddenly thought of Katsuya.

Katsuya always went grocery shopping after work, made dinner for both of them and waited for Shio. Of course, Shio had never said he wanted to eat dinner together. But it bothered him to think that Katsuya would be waiting at home for him like a puppy. Katsuya would probably be expecting him home again tonight. It also bothered him to think that he would be making Katsuya wait up for him with food he wouldn't be able to eat, so he tried calling home. There was no answer. Finally, the answering machine beeped, so he figured Katsuya wasn't home yet.

He suddenly realized that he didn't even know Katsuya's cell phone number, so he had no choice but to leave a message at home. "I'm going to be home late tonight, so I don't need any dinner," he said, and then hung up. As he did so, he wondered *why* he was even doing this. Katsuya took it upon himself to do these things, and he wouldn't listen to Shio when he refused, so why was Shio the one leaving the message? It must mean he had *really* begun to follow Katsuya's pace.

"Oh well," Shio muttered, smiling.

Surprisingly, it wasn't that bad living with someone else. He hated having someone tag along and meddle in his affairs, and tried to avoid other people at all cost, but he had begun to think that having a roommate wasn't so bad. Of course, that was probably limited to people who were like Katsuya—honest, quiet and good-natured.

After having a great dinner with his client, he got home at around 11:00 p.m. Work had gone smoothly, and he was a little drunk, so he was in a great mood that night.

"I'm home!" It was rare for him to call out like that, so Katsuya greeted him with surprise.

"Welcome home, Shio-san. You're in a good mood tonight."

"Work went well today. So, did you get my message?" Shio asked, and looked towards the dining room table. There wasn't the familiar plastic-wrapped food on the table, so it looked like he had.

"Yes, I got it. That was the first time you've ever left me a message that you were going to be late. I was so happy!"

"Happy?" *From just one phone call?* Shio thought.

Shio turned around as Katsuya spoke and saw that his roommate was grinning like a child.

"Yeah, because you contacted me first!" Katsuya said. "Up until now, I've always been the one to start conversations with you. But you called *me!* I'm so happy!"

For some reason, hearing that made Shio feel like he had been a terrible person, and it made him uneasy. "Oh, is that right?"

"Yes!" Katsuya said cheerfully.

"Oh, well. You've already eaten, right? There's some whiskey on that shelf over there, will you get it? You drink, don't you?"

"Yes, but..."

"Drink with me, then."

He lined up the whiskey bottle and glasses on the living room table. Katsuya got some ice from the freezer, then sat down on the sofa with a nervous look on his face. He was probably surprised at this sudden invitation. Up until now, Shio had only treated him coldly, so it was understandable that Katsuya would be cautious at suddenly being treated in such a friendly manner.

Shio smiled at the thought. However, the one who was the most surprised was Shio himself. As he poured the whiskey into some ice water, he wondered about his own change of heart. "Do you usually drink a lot?" he asked as he handed Katsuya a glass.

"No, but I'll drink enough to keep you company."

"You work in the Sales Department, right? You'll be entertaining clients a lot soon, so you'd better get used to drinking a lot."

"Yes, Hatanaka-san told me the same thing. I'm prepared for that." As Katsuya quickly brought the glass to his mouth, the ice cubes clinked against each other.

Shio also quietly sipped his drink. The curtains

were drawn back, and the night-time scenery of Tokyo stretched out seemingly forever beyond the glass.

The alcohol and silence brought a comfortable sense of relief to his tired body. He stared absentmindedly out the window at the view.

Katsuya followed his gaze and said, "It was so bright outside, I wanted to open the curtains."

"Bright? But it's night time."

"It's bright to me. Where I'm from, it's always pitch black at night. I mean, you can see the stars, but they're not nearly as bright as Tokyo's neon lights."

"Now that I think about it, the curtains are always open, aren't they?" Shio realized that lately, they had always been open when he came home at night.

"Well, this room is so large. If the curtains aren't open, it suddenly seems so closed in. So I just decided to keep them open. The view at night beyond the glass just sparkles and is so beautiful...it's even bright enough that I can watch TV without having to turn on any lights."

What a weirdo, Shio thought as he stole a glance at Katsuya's face. He had never once thought that Tokyo looked beautiful at night. He was so used to the scenery that it just looked like a regular city landscape to him. "The night sky in the country was much more beautiful."

"Hm?"

"It was only for that one summer, but I still remember how the night sky looked that summer in the country."

Why? Why was he remembering things about the country that he had never really thought about before?

Maybe it was because Katsuya had been there, too, that those faint memories had begun to rise to the surface again.

"That was the first time we met..." Katsuya murmured, narrowing his eyes nostalgically, as if he was remembering that time.

"It was. But we barely talked at all," Shio said as he emptied his glass.

Katsuya smiled bitterly and replied, "That's true, but it made a big impression on me. Kazuki and I played together all day, and without fail, you'd come to get him when it got dark outside. I don't have any siblings, and my parents were always busy working, so I was so jealous of Kazuki that he had such a kind older brother like you."

"I think you saved me in a way, too. Kazuki didn't want to leave Tokyo, and he threw a huge tantrum before we went to our uncle's house. He wouldn't stop crying. But since he had made such a good friend there, he didn't put up much of a fuss after that," Shio said casually, but it was the first Katsuya had ever heard of it.

His eyes widened and he looked at Shio. "Kazuki didn't want to leave Tokyo?"

"Yeah."

"But I thought you had come to visit your uncle for summer vacation? Or was it because of something else?" Katsuya hadn't yet realized that he was about to trespass on private territory once again.

Normally, Shio would refuse to answer such a personal question, but this time, he strangely was able to answer honestly. "Well, it wasn't just going on a normal summer vacation. There was someone in our family who was really sick, and they had to have surgery. It wouldn't have been good to have a loud child around that needed constant attention, so we were sent off to the country."

"So, you had to leave your parents?"

"Yeah. And he was pretty close to them."

"Um, Shio-san..." Katsuya mumbled, placing his glass on the table. The ice had melted.

"Hm?"

"Can I ask you something? If it's too personal, just tell me. But I've been wondering about it ever since I was little."

"What is it? I'll decide if I'll answer it or not after you ask me." He was a little intrigued about what Katsuya's question could be.

"Well, you're older than Kazuki, right? But why does Kazuki's name have the character for 'one' in it? I've always thought that was strange. Usually that character is only used in names of children who are the oldest."

Oh, that. Shio was used to being asked that question, and gave Katsuya a teasing look. "Is it unnatural for the younger brother to have the character for 'one' in his name?"

"No, I was just wondering if there was some kind of special meaning behind it. If there was, I'd feel weird asking Kazuki about it, so I've never asked him."

"Haven't you ever considered that both Kazuki and I are the oldest sons?"

Katsuya was stumped.

Shio explained further. "If two families become

one, sometimes the child who was previously the oldest son becomes the youngest. But you can't just change your name because of that."

"Oh, I'm sorry. So then, you and Kazuki aren't...?" *Real brothers?* Kazuki didn't finish his sentence. He suddenly realized he might have just asked something bad, and a look of regret came across his face.

This guy is so sincere it's almost sad, Shio thought. He stared at Katsuya's pitiful face. Just as Soga had said, he was a rare find these days, honest and pure. He was almost *too* honest and pure. "No, we're real brothers." It was too sad to tease him anymore.

Katsuya raised his surprised face and nodded, so Shio figured he might as well tell him the real story.

"You're right. The character for 'one' is usually only used in the name of the oldest child. Our father was also the oldest, and his name was Kazuo. So his name had the character for 'one' in it, too. When our mother was pregnant with Kazuki, our father died in an accident. When Kazuki was born, Mom thought he looked so much like our father that she wanted to use a character from his name in Kazuki's. So that's why."

"I see..."

"So it is kind of strange, but it's not like we were hiding anything. The explanation is pretty simple."

Katsuya was satisfied with the explanation that Kazuki had just inherited a character from his father's name.

Shio suddenly remembered something. "Oh, that's right. Give me your cell phone number. Just in case I need to call you."

"Oh, okay." Katsuya noisily ran to his room and brought back his cell phone. He showed Shio his number, and Shio entered it into his cell phone. After pressing a few buttons, Katsuya's phone began to ring.

Katsuya quickly answered the call. "Hello?"

"This is my number. If you ever need anything, call me," Shio said, and hung up. Putting his cell phone in his pocket, he looked at Katsuya. The other man was staring back at him, his face flushed with emotion.

Chapter 5

"Hey! How's it going?" Katsuya had returned to the office after visiting clients all morning, and had his mouth full with a rice ball, when someone slapped him on the back. Trying not to choke on his food, he coughed and turned around to see President Soga standing before him, in a great mood.

"Oh, it's going well. Thank you."

"Is Ozawa bullying you? He's a bit strange, so he can be hard to get along with."

Katsuya personally thought President Soga was much weirder than Shio, but he just smiled. "Not at all. Things are going well."

Lately, Shio had been a lot more sociable, and the stubbornness he had had when they first moved in together seemed to have disappeared. They ate breakfast together, and when they had free time, they would watch TV or DVDs together. They even exchanged normal conversation like friends. Unlike before, it seemed natural now. The nervous mood they had between them at first was gone. Their life together had transitioned to a peaceful, quiet existence.

Soga said Shio was hard to get along with, but it was only that way at first. Underneath his shrewd mask, Shio had been hiding a quiet and kind personality.

"Well, I'm glad to hear it," Soga said. "I'm sure

it's been an inconvenience, but it's only temporary, after all. As soon as we get proper company housing, you have first priority. Just wait a little longer."

"Temporary?" That was the first Katsuya had heard of it.

Ignoring Katsuya, Soga continued. "Ah, that's right! After work today, we're throwing a welcoming party."

"What? We already had one, though." There had been one about a week earlier with the Sales and Human Resources Departments. Katsuya was sure President Soga had been there...

Soga replied, as if it was completely obvious, "No, this time we're having it with the Systems Development Department. They just hired some new employees yesterday, so you can meet them, too."

"I see..."

"Ask someone from H.R. for specifics, okay? Well, I'm busy, so I'll see you later!" After saying everything he wanted to say, Soga left like a gust of wind.

"Another welcoming party..." Even though they just had one, now Katsuya had to go to another one. He wasn't happy that he wouldn't be able to fix dinner that night, but it was a company event so he had no choice.

At any rate, he figured he should probably let Shio know that he would be home late, so he took out his cell phone. It was his first time calling Shio, and he was a little nervous that his roommate might be annoyed that Katsuya was going out of his way to contact him over something like this.

"Didn't you already have a welcoming party the other day?" Shio echoed Katsuya's words to Soga earlier. Katsuya explained to him that this time it was with the Systems Development Department.

"Soga-san always thinks up stuff like this. He's so weird. As long as he has an excuse to drink alcohol, it doesn't matter what the occasion is."

"He kind of said the same thing about you," Katsuya said, chuckling.

"What do you mean?" Shio asked.

"You both said each other was weird. He asked if you were hard to get along with."

"He's saying a bunch of nonsense again." Shio clicked his tongue in exasperation. Just imagining what his face must look like at that moment made Katsuya laugh.

"So anyway, like I said, I'll be late tonight. I don't think I'll be able to make dinner, so go ahead and eat without me."

"Don't worry about me. It's not like you're my personal chef, you know. I'll think of something, so just have fun."

"But I pretty much am your personal chef..."

"Well then, you're fired!" Shio said sharply, and hung up. However, Katsuya knew that that was just Shio trying to be funny, so he was a bit happy at the other man's protest.

He had to go visit clients with Hatanaka later that afternoon. Lately, he had gotten used to his job. At first, he felt like he was just Hatanaka's assistant, but lately, he had been able to share his own ideas during meetings with clients. He was a lot more familiar with his clients than before, and there were times when they bounced project ideas off each other. He realized that his skills as a salesman were growing, and his job was starting to get more interesting.

Hatanaka had told him, "Soon, you'll have to go around to clients by yourself, so you better prepare yourself!"

Katsuya looked forward to the day when he would be recognized as a full-fledged member of the company. They returned to the office after 6:00 p.m. and then headed towards the location of the party. It was at a nearby *yakiniku* restaurant. There were already many people there from Systems Development that Katsuya had never met before. They worked on different floors, so they didn't have many opportunities to interact. A large group of women arrived after Katsuya, and he found out that they had recently joined the Systems Development Department.

Katsuya sat in between a group of women. Yoshimi, a young woman around the same age as him, offered him some drinks. They both exchanged phone numbers. He was having a lot of fun for the first time in a long time.

After the restaurant closed at 9:00 p.m., the girls dragged Katsuya to a bar. Around 10, he was finally making his way home. The girls were really excited about going to another bar, but he somehow escaped. He staggered towards the train station, grateful that tomorrow was a Saturday.

Katsuya wasn't very good at holding his liquor. If

he drank too much, he wouldn't feel well, and there was always a nasty hangover waiting for him the next day. He knew he had to wake up early to make breakfast, so he hoped he wouldn't have one this time.

As he reached the condo, he looked up and saw that there were already lights on in their room. It looked like Shio was already home.

Lately, Shio had been coming home around 9:00 p.m., so he probably had come home again at the same time. He was probably watching TV or reading. It was usually Katsuya who greeted Shio when he came home, so he was a little excited to be on the opposite end that night.

"I'm home!" he called out as he stepped inside, and noticed some unfamiliar sneakers by the door. He tilted his head, confused. Shio's leather shoes were already there, so they couldn't be his. He slowly continued down the hallway. The noise from the TV escaped from the door leading to the living room.

"Shio-san?" Katsuya slowly opened the door. Sitting on the sofa beside Shio was a young man he didn't recognize. Katsuya stared at the young man's hand, which was resting intimately on Shio's knee. "Oh, do you have a guest?" He finally managed to say despite his bewilderment.

Shio quickly pushed the man's hand away and stood up. "Welcome home. This isn't really a guest, this is my younger brother."

"Younger brother?" Katsuya was shocked. This was the first time he had heard of Shio having a brother other than Kazuki. He was sure Kazuki had always said he only had one brother, ever since they had first met.

"Yes. This is my younger brother, Takamasa. He's a college student." Takamasa remained seated on the sofa, giving Katsuya only a quick glance and a slight bow.

Shio said this was his brother, but he didn't resemble either him or Kazuki. Also, he looked more like a high school student than a college student. He had an intelligent face. Katsuya could tell from his eyes that he was a headstrong person.

"Nice to meet you. I'm Narita. Shio-san has helped me out a lot." Katsuya introduced himself.

However, Takamasa ignored him and said, "I thought you were living alone? Why do you have a roommate?"

"I just told you. His company housing fell through. We couldn't let him live in a hotel, so it was an emergency situation. The president made the decision; I had no choice in the matter."

"But you're an investor in the company. Plus, you're an executive. Why did you let yourself be ordered around?"

"It wasn't like that. I was just trying to think of the best solution for the company. As soon as the new company housing is ready, he's leaving anyway." Even though it looked like Takamasa was reluctantly satisfied with Shio's explanation, Katsuya was not.

"Shio-san..."

Shio shook his head slightly, as if to silence Katsuya. Katsuya wasn't sure if Shio had seen his uneasy expression or not, but Katsuya understood that

the gesture was a sign that Shio didn't want him to say anything anymore about this matter.

He withdrew to his room and changed his clothes, feeling a little gloomy.

He had somehow sobered up, and instinctively had a bad feeling about Takamasa showing up.

Returning to the living room, he saw that Shio had sat back down on the sofa with Takamasa. They chatted while they watched TV. It's not that they didn't *seem* like brothers, but Katsuya thought it was a little over the top how closely Takamasa snuggled against Shio. If they were brothers, shouldn't they have a more candid relationship like he had with Kazuki? Takamasa wasn't a child anymore. It was unbelievable.

Katsuya suddenly realized he was feeling hostility towards Takamasa. Even though it was normal for brothers to be close, he was angry about it. Actually, he was more *jealous* than angry. Takamasa was snuggling up to Shio. Touching Shio. Takamasa was doing all the things Katsuya wanted to, but couldn't. Seeing it right before his eyes made him extremely jealous.

However, he shook off those thoughts. How could he be jealous? There was no way he could tell Shio his feelings now. He made some coffee and set it down on the table in front of them.

"Thanks," Shio said, but Takamasa took the cup silently, as if he expected to be treated like this.

Katsuya sat down at the dining room table, just to get away from the sofa where the two men were sitting.

"Hey, Shio. Can I spend the night here?" Takamasa said, loudly enough for Katsuya to hear.

"Absolutely not."

"Why not?"

"Because I don't live alone anymore. This is Narita-kun's company housing, so people who don't work for the company aren't allowed to stay overnight here."

"What if Narita-san says I can?"

"That's not the point."

However, Takamasa ignored Shio, and turned towards Katsuya. "Narita-san, you don't mind right? It's been so long since I've seen my brother..." he said in a goading tone of voice.

"No...if Shio-san...if Ozawa-san says no, then it's probably not okay," Katsuya said.

Takamasa glared at him harshly. "But I came all the way here, and now you're kicking me out? It's late!"

"I'll take you home," Shio said, standing up. He retrieved his car keys from the sideboard.

Takamasa turned away. "No. I wanna stay here."

"Takamasa. Don't be so childish," Shio said calmly.

"But I haven't seen you in so long! You never come home; you never even call me! I've waited so long to see you, but all you do is ignore me!" Takamasa raised his voice angrily.

"I've been busy with work."

Takamasa's eyes filled with tears. It seemed like he really meant what he had said. He had been waiting for Shio, his desperate protests proved that.

"Shio-san, it doesn't really matter to..."

Shio didn't want to hear it and interrupted Katsuya. "Come on, I'll drive you home. Let's go, Takamasa." He quickly left the living room with car keys in hand. It seemed like Shio was really determined to take his brother home.

At the sound of the front door closing, Takamasa raised his tear-stained face. He glared at Katsuya for a while and said rudely, "You better hurry up and move out of here."

He slammed the door violently. At that sound, Katsuya relaxed his shoulders and sighed deeply. He didn't understand why Takamasa had glared at him like that, or why he had told him to move out. Did he really care who his brother lived with *that* much? He also couldn't figure out why Shio was so dead-set against letting him stay overnight. Katsuya didn't like the idea of having to kick out his brother, who had come all the way here to see him.

Because even if Takamasa was childish or selfish, he was still Shio's brother. But it looked like Shio had no desire to let him stay overnight.

Katsuya was left alone in the deathly silent room, so he began clearing the coffee cups. He decided he would ask Shio about Takamasa when he returned home. He knew full well that Shio disliked people nosing around in his personal affairs, but Katsuya couldn't stand not knowing what was going on.

He felt that if he didn't ask Shio himself, he would never understand his roommate. He didn't like not knowing. Not knowing about Shio. Katsuya had had no idea that Shio had another younger brother. He also didn't understand the way Shio treated him. Besides, he really wanted to know what Shio meant by saying they were only roommates because it had been an emergency situation, and that as soon as company housing was available, Katsuya would move out.

* * *

Apparently, he had nodded off to sleep on the sofa. He felt something shaking his shoulder back and forth, as he opened his eyes sleepily.

"Morning," Shio's comforting voice said. He had been the one shaking Katsuya's shoulder.

Katsuya suddenly became conscious of his shoulder that had been touched. No matter what form, it was the first time Shio had touched him. His heart soared.

"I'm sorry. I thought I'd wait for you to get home, but I must have fallen asleep!" As he looked around the bright room, even his sleepy mind realized it wasn't night anymore.

"It's alright. I didn't tell you when I'd be back, so I guess I made you wait up. Takamasa wouldn't calm down last night, so I ended up staying at my parents' house."

"Oh, I see..." The clock on the wall read 9:00 a.m. Even though he had stayed at his parents' house, Shio still looked a little exhausted. "Shio-san, are you okay?"

"Hm? Why do you ask?"

"You look like you're in pain or something..."

Katsuya peered at his face with a worried expression, but Shio smiled at him reassuredly.

"I'm okay. I'm going to put some coffee on. Want some?"

"No, I'll make it."

"No, it's okay. Go wash your face. Let me make the coffee today." Shio's kindness made Katsuya happy. He went to the bathroom and washed his face, but then remembered he hadn't taken a bath the night before, so he took a quick shower.

Drying his wet hair with a towel, he returned to the living room. Shio was already there, drinking coffee.

"So, did your brother make it home safely?"

"Yeah."

"Takamasa-san, was it? Honestly, I had no idea that you and Kazuki had another brother. He never mentioned it to me."

"Oh..."

"I'm sorry if I'm being rude. But if I don't find out, I won't be able to relax..."

Shio poured him some coffee, and Katsuya took the cup from him. Shio tilted his head. "Kazuki never mentioned him?"

"No, never. I'm pretty sure Kazuki even said there were only two of you, so that's why I'm so confused," Katsuya answered honestly.

"I guess so," Shio murmured.

Maybe there was some kind of circumstances? Katsuya thought.

Noticing Katsuya's worried look, Shio's

expression softened and he began to speak. "Before, remember when I told you about the meaning of Kazuki's name? I used the example of two families coming together to be one, and the oldest sibling suddenly becomes the youngest?"

"I remember." After hearing that example, Katsuya had inadvertently doubted that Shio and Kazuki were real brothers for a moment. But he was relieved to learn that it was just a misunderstanding.

"Well, that's how Takamasa is. After my dad died, my mom remarried. My stepfather is Takamasa's dad. So even though he had been the oldest in his previous family, now he's the youngest after Kazuki and me."

Ohhh, Katsuya thought. *So the example Shio used was true, after all.*

"So, that summer we met...at that time, Takamasa was very sick and had been hospitalized for a long time. Our parents really had their hands full, so they sent Kazuki and me to our uncle's house. Takamasa has always had a weak body. Maybe he was too spoiled because of it, and that's why he turned out to be so selfish."

"He really loves you, doesn't he?" Katsuya remembered how Takamasa cried the night before. He had cried and yelled after Shio had left him. It was clear how he felt towards Shio after seeing that desperation.

"He's really attached to me. He's not a bad kid, but he just needs to grow up and stop being so clingy."

"Does he live at home with your parents?"

"Yeah. He had surgery, so he's pretty much healthy now. But my parents still worry about him, so they don't want to be away from him. However, Takamasa wants to move out, and he used to come here all the time."

"He was insisting on staying here, too..." *If he wanted to stay so bad, why not just let him?* Katsuya thought. But that wasn't for him to decide. He instinctively knew that he shouldn't meddle with the brothers.

"If I let him stay one night, he starts to ask if he can move in, so I never let him stay anymore. This is my place, and it was too much trouble having him stay here. My parents would tell me to bring him back home, and then Takamasa would insist that he wanted to live here and wouldn't listen to anyone. So I was in a lose-lose situation. I asked Soga-san for advice, and he recommended that I move into company housing and say it was reserved for employees living away from their families. Since non-employees can't live in that kind of company housing, I used that as an excuse to tell Takamasa he couldn't move in with me. So that's why I moved here."

"Oh, so that's why..." President Soga had helped him move into the condo, so that was why Shio couldn't refuse his request to have Katsuya live with him. However, if they had passed off the condo as company housing that was reserved for people who lived away from their families, that lie had been destroyed when Katsuya moved in. Those people only live alone. Takamasa probably picked up on that the night before.

"Even last night when I went home, it was a lot of trouble. All he did was complain about you. When I said

I was going home, he just wouldn't let me go."

Katsuya remained silent.

The image of Takamasa clinging to Shio appeared in his mind. If he always cried and carried on like that, he probably got even the cold Shio to give in once in a while. Just thinking of it made Katsuya's chest throb painfully. Takamasa was trying to have Shio all to himself. Even if he was Shio's younger brother, his presence still disturbed Katsuya.

*Ahh...*Katsuya thought. He loved Shio now more than he did before he had come to Tokyo. Since they started living together, he had begun to get to know a new side of Shio that was different from the memories he had had of him. He wanted to know more about Shio.

At the same time, he wanted to tell Shio about himself. He wanted Shio to touch him again. But no matter how much he wished for it, he knew it was only one-sided.

Suddenly quiet, Katsuya stared at his coffee while Shio watched him. He felt troubled by all the feelings inside of him. He sighed sadly, and felt Shio looking at him from the side. Finally, Shio spoke. "Since we have the day off..."

Katsuya looked up. *What about it?* he thought.

"Let's go out to the city. You still haven't been sightseeing in Tokyo yet. I'll go with you." Katsuya held his breath in surprise. He had never been invited out like this before. Shio was unsure how to react to Katsuya's surprise, so he just stood up and said in a cheerful voice, "Let's go."

Chapter 6

As they left the train station, they joined a huge crowd. Probably because it was Saturday, there were tourists left and right. Katsuya, who was walking beside Shio, had a look of surprise on his face. After they walked for a little bit, they could see the big lantern of the Kaminarimon Gate, the symbol of Asakusa.

"Wow..." Katsuya said quietly, with his eyes shining. When they had left the condo, they had tried to decide where to go, but Katsuya couldn't think of anything, so Shio had decided to take him sightseeing in Asakusa.

If they went there, they'd see lots of tourist attractions that Katsuya probably had only heard of, so then he could tell people he had been to them.

After passing through the Kaminarimon Gate, the road leading to the temple stretched about 300 meters until the Houzoumon Gate. Famous shops lined the road of the shrine, selling rice cookies, *ningyouyaki* cakes and various souvenirs.

As they window-shopped, groups of tourists milled around them. There were a lot of foreigners around, and Katsuya realized once again that these were the kinds of tourists that came to Tokyo.

"It's been a long time since I've been to Asakusa. The last time I came here, I was still a child," Shio said as they walked up the crowded park to a shrine. Katsuya, who seemed to have cheered up, nodded.

"I guess if there are always so many tourists, it would be difficult for locals to come very often."

"But when we saw the Kaminarimon Gate, it really brought back memories. Maybe that's just how Japanese are."

"I know what you mean, that feeling. Maybe it's because I've seen Asakusa so much on TV, but I feel kind of nostalgic, too. Even though this is my first time here." Katsuya smiled cheerfully.

Shio was relieved to see him smile. He had been worried that Katsuya had been feeling down because of Takamasa.

They went inside an accessory shop, and Katsuya bought a boxwood comb and leather wallet. "Since I'm here, I think I'd like to buy some souvenirs to send to my parents. I haven't bought them anything since I started my new job."

"Did your parents say anything when you told them you were going to work here?"

"I think they were worried about me going so far away at first, but in the end, I think they were okay with it. It's my life, so they told me I could do what I wanted."

"Your parents sound great."

"They are. I'm really thankful."

There aren't many people who could easily say they were thankful for their parents nowadays, Shio thought kindly as Katsuya clutched the souvenirs to his chest as if they were very precious to him.

After they passed through the Houzoumon Gate, they entered the compound of Kannon, the goddess of mercy. They entered a spacious area, and they both looked up at the vast blue sky. There was the constant smell of incense, so now that they were out in the open, they were flooded with a sense of openness.

Shio and Katsuya both paid their respects in the inner building of the temple. After that, they wandered around aimlessly for a while.

Luckily, the weather was great. Katsuya began feeling a little warm, so he took off his jacket and threw it over his arm.

"So, how is Asakusa?" Shio asked.

"I'm glad we came. I guess if you come to Tokyo, you definitely have to visit Asakusa."

"Didn't you come here on any field trips?"

"No. In junior high, we went to Kansai. I thought maybe we'd go during high school, but we ended up going overseas. Nowadays, there are lots of people who take family vacations to Disneyland, so I guess it's not popular to visit Tokyo anymore."

"Overseas, huh? I did a home stay in Australia during high school." They had a great time chatting about their various field trips. Their hometowns were completely different, so the different local field trips they had were really interesting.

"Well, I'm starving," Shio suddenly said.

"Yeah, it's past lunchtime," Katsuya said, glancing at his watch. They had decided to eat brunch earlier, but they hadn't had a proper meal yet. Unfortunately, all the restaurants in Asakusa were packed.

"Let's ride the ferry to Odaiba. The food's really great there," Shio said as they bought small packages of *ningyouyaki* cakes at a shop off the temple path. Katsuya's eyes widened as if he had never heard the word before.

"A ferry?" Katsuya looked so confused that Shio laughed.

"Yeah, you know, a boat."

They left the shop and returned to the Kaminarimon Gate. As they walked a little more, they saw the Azuma Bridge and the ferry depot station. There was a crowd of tourists waiting for the boat's departure, and it seemed that there was a standard "Asakusa to Odaiba" tour.

"Wow, this is *so* cool!"

The boat was named Himiko, and its exterior looked just like a spaceship. A manga artist named Leiji Matsumoto had designed this strange ship, and Katsuya's eyes sparkled like a child's.

Inside, they bought some drinks and sat down. As they picked at their *ningyouyaki* cakes, they gazed out at the view. The bright sun reflected off the waves Himiko splashed up. It was beautiful.

Sitting next to Shio, Katsuya stared out of the boat's window.

The boat traveled down the Sumida River and entered the Tokyo Bay, heading for Odaiba Beach Park.

"Shio-san..." Katsuya said hesitantly. He had been quiet for some time, looking outside and drinking.

"Hm?"

"Are you sure it's not bothering you that I'm

living with you?"

"What?" Honestly, Shio was confused. *Why is he asking me this now*? he thought. He didn't know how to answer Katsuya.

"I know you only did it because President Soga made you. I'm just not sure how long I can let you do this favor for me."

"Why are you asking me this all of a sudden?" Shio asked.

No matter how it had been at first, both he and Katsuya were starting to get used to their lives together.

His heart had been stubborn when his comfortable, solitary lifestyle had been interrupted, but after living with Katsuya, he finally felt like he had attained an even more comfortable lifestyle. Also, he liked being with Katsuya. He wasn't sure why, but lately, Katsuya's presence had become natural—like air.

"Yesterday, you told Takamasa-san that we had become roommates just because it had been an emergency situation, and that I'd move out of the condo as soon as they found new company housing." As Katsuya said this, his face returned to the same miserable expression he had before. Slightly sad, slightly pained.

"That's because...I just said that to shut Takamasa up!" Shio exclaimed. He didn't actually mean what he said. If he hadn't said it, Takamasa would have kept going on and on. He had only said it as an excuse to calm his brother down.

It was true that it had been an emergency situation. But that didn't mean he thought Katsuya was a nuisance and wanted him to move out. It didn't look like Katsuya was convinced at Shio's explanation.

"Are you sure? Even if Takamasa wasn't in the picture, isn't that how things are? That's what the president said. That Shio-san's condo was only a temporary living arrangement, and that before long, he'd arrange proper company housing for me. But I never thought of the condo as temporary."

"That's because Soga-san was probably just concerned about you. It's his fault that you had this inconvenience forced on you in the first place."

"I never thought this was an inconvenience. I like living with you," Katsuya said, biting his lip, watching Shio's reaction closely.

Oh, I see, Shio thought. Katsuya had begun to like his lifestyle just as much as he had, he realized, and relaxed his shoulders.

"So do I. I like living with you, too."

"Shio-san..."

"I know I said some harsh things in the beginning, but ever since living with you, I've come to think that having a roommate is kind of nice. There's always someone there to greet me when I come home. A hot meal is waiting for me. It's such a relief to come home to that after a hard day." He was a little embarrassed at being so open with his feelings, but Katsuya wouldn't know if he didn't tell him. Shio felt that he should be as open with Katsuya as the other man was being with him.

Katsuya was silent. However, his expression had completely changed to a look that seemed half confused and half thrilled at Shio's words. Shio wanted to turn that expression to one of pure happiness, so he decided to tell him everything.

"But I only think that because you're my roommate. It's really fun being with you."

"Shio-san..." Katsuya's face turned red. He noticed that Shio was looking at him kindly, and quickly turned his face away, trying to hide his embarrassment. Shio couldn't help but think he was adorable.

The ferry had almost reached Odaiba. Looking up at the large buildings he could see out the window, Katsuya narrowed his eyes.

After they got off the ferry, they walked around Odaiba Beach Park aimlessly. The weather was great, so there were lots of families and couples on the beach.

The view of the quiet inlet was really something. Katsuya nodded happily while Shio pointed out the Rainbow Bridge and other sights on the opposite shore.

Inside the park, there were lots of decks and benches. They finally sat down on an empty bench. They were surrounded by couples.

Katsuya seemed to realize that and let out a chuckle. "It looks like everyone's on a date."

"At night, I'm sure there will be even more. The city at night is really beautiful, so this is a popular date spot."

"Oh, I see. I'm sure the view of Rainbow Bridge is beautiful at night."

"Do you want to come see it?" After they ate, they could kill a little time, and it might be fun to see the city at night. Shio had casually suggested it, but Katsuya shook his head and looked troubled.

"But there will only be couples there. I'm not sure I want to."

"Don't worry about it. Just think of this as a date, too," Shio blurted out, and then realized what he had said. A date between two men? Shio panicked and looked at Katsuya's face. He seemed surprised at Shio's words, but also happy. Katsuya smiled cheerfully, and Shio suddenly felt restless.

He abruptly stood up and urged Katsuya to follow him. "Well, let's go eat."

"Wait, Shio-san." Katsuya noisily ran after him. Shio stopped and looked behind him to see Katsuya trailing behind him like a puppy. He smiled and thought that it *did* kind of feel like a date.

* * *

They ate a late lunch at a cafe terrace that faced the park. Maybe it was because they didn't really eat a proper breakfast and had wandered all around Asakusa and Odaiba, but they were both starving. They quickly ate their steak.

After their meal, they ordered some coffee. As they drank, they gazed out the window at the view of the ocean colored by the setting sun.

In the comfortable silence, Shio felt somehow relaxed.

It seemed that Katsuya felt the same, and he stared out the window with his chin resting on his hands, lost in thought.

They didn't need to speak—just spending time

together was comfortable.

"Narita-kun."

Katsuya looked up as Shio called his name. He said hesitantly, "You can just call me Katsuya, since I call you Shio-san."

"Oh, okay."

"You can still call me Narita-kun at work, though."

"Okay, then, Katsuya."

"Yes?" Katsuya shyly answered.

"What if...what if Soga-san really finds new company housing for you? What would you do?"

"Well, that's up to you. I'm just a freeloader after all, so I'll do whatever you want me to. But if there's new company housing and you tell me I can still stay, then I wouldn't want to move anywhere else."

"Well, I'm not sure what Soga-san is planning to do, but I do want you to stay."

"Really?"

"Yes, really." Shio truly meant what he said. He wanted to be with Katsuya. Even if they found the ultimate company housing, he'd still want him to stay at the condo.

"If that's what you want, then that's what I'll do."

"Well, then, it's decided. If Soga-san arranges new company housing, we'll both insist that you stay with me."

"Shio-san, thank you so much! I'm so happy!" Katsuya was all smiles. Shio had been waiting for that smile.

After they left the restaurant, they decided to head home. As they walked towards the train station, they enjoyed the night view of Odaiba, side by side. Katsuya smiled like he didn't have a care in the world. Encouraged by that smile, Shio felt himself smile back kindly.

Katsuya's presence was slowly growing bigger inside of him. His younger brother's friend, he was supposed to be a roommate forced on him by his company, but there was something more than that in Shio's heart. A passion he hadn't felt in a long time.

Even though he didn't understand it, he knew that he had been starving for those feelings. After changing trains, they returned to Higashinakano and went shopping at the neighborhood supermarket.

Katsuya was normally the one who bought the groceries, but Shio had suggested that they split the bill from now on. However, Shio was paying for it tonight so they stocked up.

"Oh, Shio-san, I forgot to buy lettuce."

"It's okay, we'll get it next time. We have cabbage, can you use that?"

"I guess so. I'll make a really delicious breakfast tomorrow. Shio-san, if you want to eat anything in particular, let me know."

"Okay, how about gratin? With tons of cheese on it."

They discussed it as they got off the elevator in the condo. Shio walked ahead and took his keys out of his pocket, when he suddenly saw that someone was standing outside of their condo. He stopped suddenly.

Katsuya, who was following behind him with the

grocery bags, nearly bumped into him. "Shio-san?" he said cautiously.

Shio's face hardened as he saw that Takamasa was leaning against the door to their condo with his arms crossed. He had a bad feeling about this. "Takamasa."

"You're *really* late."

"What do you mean? It's only nine."

"That's not what I mean. You've been gone ever since this morning." Apparently, Takamasa had tried to visit early that morning. It was kind of scary to think that he thought it was normal to lay in wait for so many hours.

"You waited this whole time?" Shio asked.

"I didn't know you were going to be home this late."

"Well, whatever. You're probably tired, so come in." Since he had waited so long, they couldn't just kick him out now. Also, he had been standing around outside for hours with no food; they were worried about his weak body.

Shio unlocked the door, and Takamasa followed him, with Katsuya trailing behind, carrying the groceries. He put the bags on the dining room table.

Takamasa stretched out on the sofa, exhausted. Katsuya was about to boil some water when Shio looked at him with an uneasy look on his face. "Katsuya, it's okay. Let me take care of Takamasa."

"But..."

"Just get him some bread and milk; I'm sure he's hungry."

"Well, if it's okay, I can make something small.

Eating just bread and milk won't fill him up. I'll make omelettes and soup or something."

Even though he didn't want Katsuya to go to any trouble, Shio was happy at the offer. He couldn't cook himself, so he decided to take Katsuya up on it. "Okay then, thanks." He returned to Takamasa's side. The boy's eyes were closed in exhaustion, and Shio felt his forehead. It didn't feel like he had a fever, but he was definitely weakened by fatigue. "Are you okay?" he said gently.

Takamasa opened his eyes slowly and gave an angelic smile. "Yeah, I'm okay."

"You always push yourself too hard."

"But I wanted to see you."

"You just saw me yesterday."

"But you left while I was sleeping. Even after you said we could spend the whole weekend together."

"No, *you* said that. You're really a pain, you know that? You're *way* too attached to me."

Ever since he was small, Takamasa had adored his step-brother. He had no idea why. He didn't get along at all with Shio's other brother, Kazuki. He was only close to Shio.

There were times when Takamasa's attachment to him annoyed Shio, but Takamasa had had to withstand so many surgeries and hospitalizations with his weak body. So when he showed Shio so much affection, Shio had to admit it was adorable. Even though they weren't related by blood, he felt like they were even closer than real brothers.

Katsuya was busy in the kitchen preparing

Takamasa's food. Every now and then, he would cast a worried glance at Takamasa and Shio's direction.

Shio indirectly looked at Katsuya. They had come home after spending such a fun day together, only to have Takamasa to take care of, and it made Shio feel bad.

He wanted to come home in the same mood they were in at Odaiba. There were so many more things he wanted to talk about with Katsuya.

As he stared at Katsuya, he felt someone watching him. Turning around, he saw that it was Takamasa, who was still lying on the couch.

"Where did you go today?"

Shio answered firmly, never taking his eyes off him, "Oh, Asakusa and Odaiba."

"With him?"

Him must mean Katsuya. Shio nodded. "He hadn't been sightseeing in Tokyo yet, so I just showed him around a little."

"You were together *the whole day?*" Shio was annoyed at the emphasis Takamasa put on the words "the whole day."

Without answering him, Shio calmly spoke. "After you eat, you need to go home. I'll drive you."

"No way, I'm spending the night here."

"I told you, you can't because this place belongs to the company. So non-employees can't stay overnight."

"But I'm tired already. And it's *your* fault. So you'll have to take responsibility for it."

Why was he blaming Shio? Takamasa was the one making unreasonable demands, yet he was telling

Shio it was his fault?

"You know..." He couldn't put up with it any longer, and was about to scold the little brat when Katsuya called out.

"The food is ready. Takamasa-san, come eat while it's still warm."

"Yay!" Takamasa must have sensed Shio's anger, because he leapt up in joy at the sound of Katsuya's voice. He raced to the dining table, where the food was already set out.

Takamasa gobbled up the bread, soup, omelette, and salad that had been set out before him. Shio sat down at the table, as well.

After eating, Takamasa, who had obviously been starving, told Katsuya it was delicious. Katsuya put on some coffee for him, which made him even happier. "Narita-san, you're a great cook. It was so good."

"Thanks."

"Did you take cooking classes or something?"

"Nope. My parents both worked, so I ended up helping with meals a lot. After that, I started to enjoy cooking."

"That's so cool! I've never even held a kitchen knife before!" Maybe it was because his stomach was full, but the usually shy Takamasa was quite talkative towards Katsuya.

Katsuya, looking a little confused at Takamasa's kindness, smiled shyly. He began to clear the dishes. Shio brought some plates and cups over to the sink to help him, when the phone rang.

"Shio-san, the phone's ringing."

Shio went to answer the phone. It was someone from work that needed to confirm the content of a certain document right away. Shio went to his room and pulled the document from his briefcase. He settled the matter in about five minutes.

Shio returned to the living room, but before he could return the cordless phone to the cradle, Takamasa dropped a bomb on him.

"Shio, Narita-san said I could spend night."

"What?"

"He said I looked so tired that it was okay tonight."

"No, you can't."

"I don't care what you say, I'm staying." Shio bit his lip at Takamasa's insistence. He glared at Katsuya, but it looked like he already knew Shio would be angry, and was hanging his head. He looked like he was very sorry. Takamasa had probably persuaded him with tears while Shio had been gone, or maybe Takamasa had charmed him until he eventually agreed. The boy was the kind of person who did whatever was necessary in order to get what he wanted. He clearly took advantage of Katsuya, but Shio couldn't help being angry with his roommate.

If Katsuya said it was okay, there was no way Takamasa would listen to Shio now. He tried anyway. "I'll drive you home, let's go," he repeated.

All the little brat did in response was to stick out his tongue at Shio.

Chapter 7

After Takamasa had relentlessly asked him, Katsuya had given in and meant to say, "Well, if it's okay with your brother, I don't mind if you stay," but he had been interrupted. It was just his luck. Katsuya had given in because Takamasa was Shio's brother. He couldn't take it back now. He had prefaced it by saying "If your brother says it's okay..." but Takamasa insisted that he had said "I don't care at all if you stay."

Sure enough, Shio was glaring at him furiously.

It was wrong of him to interfere in a family matter.

He tried to apologize to Shio over and over again, but it seemed like the brunt of Shio's anger was directed towards him and not Takamasa. Shio stared at him as if he was blaming him; it hurt his chest. Shio had tried to persuade Takamasa to go home, but eventually gave up on it. Takamasa was being unreasonable. Finally, Shio said, "Do whatever you want. I'll sleep on the couch, so you can have my bed," and disappeared into the bathroom.

Left alone in the living room with Takamasa, Katsuya said, "You shouldn't give your brother so much trouble," to which Takamasa immediately replied, "Shut up." Katsuya decided never to get in the middle of their affairs again.

Before long, Shio finished taking a shower and returned to the living room, where he began to get ready to sleep on the sofa.

"Takamasa, if you're so exhausted that you can't go home, you should go to bed." In spite of Shio's harsh tone, Takamasa continued to cling to him.

"I'll go to bed, but only if you sleep in bed with me. You can't get very good sleep on the sofa."

"You're not a child anymore. You're an adult; you can sleep by yourself."

"But you used to sleep with me..."

"That was then," Shio answered, extremely angry.

Takamasa realized he shouldn't make Shio angrier, so he reluctantly headed towards Shio's bedroom.

Now that it was quiet, Shio arranged a blanket and pillow on the sofa.

"Shio-san, I..." Katsuya said hesitantly. He really wanted to apologize. He'd never seen Shio so angry, and he was partly to blame for it.

Shio lay down on the couch, and faced the TV, switching it on. Without taking his eyes off the screen, he said coldly, "You should go take a bath. Don't worry about Takamasa. He'll catch a cold if he takes a bath when he's this tired."

Even though Shio had started to call Katsuya by name earlier today during their Odaiba date, he was now calling him "you" again. Katsuya was shocked. All the trust that they had built up that day had been destroyed in an instant. He was amazed that one careless slip of the tongue had made Shio this angry with him.

He couldn't say anything. He figured Shio wouldn't want to hear anything he had to say.

After taking a shower in the bathroom, he changed into his pajamas and came back out into the hallway. He could still hear the sound of the TV coming from the living room. He sighed. There was no use in worrying about it tonight, he'd try to apologize again tomorrow. With drooping shoulders, he returned to his bedroom. Even though it was still early, he laid down on his mattress anyway.

He closed his eyes and tried to go to sleep, but all he could think of was the day's events with Shio. Shio showing him around Asakusa and Odaiba, explaining all the tourist attractions.

Shio's beautiful smile had shone against the clear sky. He had been so kind to Katsuya. He had even teased him, calling it a date. The whole day had been like a dream to Katsuya.

But with one slip of the tongue, Katsuya had destroyed it all. He worriedly tossed and turned on his mattress. No matter how hard he tried, he just couldn't get to sleep. It was no use. He grabbed the alarm clock next to his pillow and looked at the glowing numbers. It was only midnight.

Katsuya jumped out of bed. He just couldn't wait until tomorrow to apologize. If Shio was still watching TV, he was probably still awake. Since he normally went to bed late, he was most likely still awake. Katsuya walked out into the hallway and listened closely. He faintly heard the sound of the television. He crept down the hall and slightly opened up the door to the living room. The light from the television screen flickered in the dark room.

Is he still awake? Katsuya wondered, and peered through to the living room. In that instant, he gasped. A dark silhouette stood out against the flickering light. Takamasa knelt beside Shio, who was lying on the couch. He touched Shio's beautiful face, leaned over, and softly kissed him on the lips.

* * *

Katsuya was thankful for the loud pachinko parlor. He hadn't slept much the night before. He couldn't apologize to Shio. He couldn't even look at his face. Takamasa acted as if he lived there. Feeling out of place, Katsuya left shortly after breakfast to go out to the city.

However, since he wasn't very familiar with the neighborhood yet, he could only go to a pachinko parlor or arcade. It was the first time he had played pachinko in Tokyo. Perhaps it was beginner's luck, but Katsuya put 10,000 yen in the machine and won 60,000 yen. But he couldn't be truly happy about winning. Because when he was on his way to apologize to Shio, he had witnessed something unimaginable—Takamasa kissing a sleeping Shio.

Truthfully, he wasn't sure if Shio had been asleep or not. But he hadn't resisted Takamasa or said anything. But the way Takamasa had gently touched Shio, Katsuya guessed that Shio had been sleeping.

But, how should he act now? Takamasa had stolen a kiss from his sleeping brother. A kiss between two men. Two step-brothers. Katsuya's mind raced. He wondered if they had always had that kind of relationship, and began to imagine all kinds of unpleasant things.

When he had woken up that morning, he couldn't even look at Shio's face. But it didn't matter. Shio had ignored him coldly, anyway.

Takamasa had taken advantage of that hole in their relationship. He had been in high spirits that morning, following Shio around and talking to him non-stop. Shio's demeanor towards him had softened since the night before, and he was actually paying attention to him.

It was painful. Katsuya couldn't bear watching the two of them like that. So that's why he had left, even with nothing to do. All he could do was kill time at the pachinko parlor. The rattle of the pachinko balls and the clatter of the sound of winning matches somehow took Katsuya's mind off his sadness.

After leaving the pachinko parlor, he went to a fast food restaurant. He ordered a hamburger and soda, and then sat down at a window side table. Taking out his cell phone, he dialed Kazuki's number.

"Hello, Kazuki? It's me, Katsuya."

"Oh, haven't talked to you in a while. So, what's up? Are things going well with Shio?" Kazuki asked.

Now that Katsuya thought about it, he hadn't seen Kazuki since that night at the bar. He had thought that he only had Kazuki to rely on when he first came to Tokyo, but now it seemed like he was somehow getting used to his life here without his friend's help.

"I guess so," he answered.

"That's a weird answer. Well, whatever. So what's up?"

"Not much...So I guess you and Shio-san have another brother?"

"Oh, that idiot? Has Takamasa been bothering you?" Katsuya had just tested the waters, but Kazuki's response was pretty forceful.

"I didn't know you had a step-brother, so I was really surprised when I heard about it."

"We only became siblings because of my mom's second marriage. I don't think of him as a brother at all."

"So you don't get along?"

"I don't know why, but ever since we were little, he has always disliked me, just as much as he's been attached to Shio. He just pretends to be good in front of Shio."

It didn't seem like Takamasa was trying to be good lately. But it was clear that he was attached to Shio, from the things he said and the way he behaved.

"He suddenly came to the condo and insisted that he stay the night. Shio-san couldn't control him," Katsuya confessed.

"He's always like that. When Shio was a junior in college, he wanted to get an apartment by himself, then Takamasa threw a fit and said he wanted to move in, too. He was only in high school at that time, so my parents wouldn't hear of it. He finally gave up on it, but I guess it started up again."

"So it's happened before, then."

"Yeah. Shio still spoils him, and Takamasa knows it, so he thinks that means he can do anything he wants. Once he said something really terrible to me, and I just kind of snapped and kicked him. Shio got so pissed that he punched me. I couldn't believe it. That was the only time he had ever hit me."

Katsuya couldn't even imagine Shio punching Kazuki. It made him remember how Shio would come get him that summer when it got dark.

"Hey..."

"Hm?"

He felt a little weird asking this, but felt like he wouldn't be able to relax if he didn't.

"Does Takamasa-san like Shio-san?" he asked hesitantly.

"Of course he likes him. Can't you tell?"

"That's not what I mean..." Not *that* kind of like. Katsuya meant to ask if Takamasa liked Shio romantically. He decided not to question his friend any further.

If Kazuki hadn't noticed what he really meant, there was no sense in spelling it out for him. Even if Takamasa did have feelings for Shio, Kazuki probably didn't want to know about it. Anyway, he decided he wasn't going to get in the middle of these brothers.

"Then what do you mean?" Kazuki wanted to know the rest, but Katsuya somehow avoided answering him and hung up the phone.

He knew it. Takamasa hated Kazuki just as fiercely as he was obsessed with Shio. Also, it seemed like Shio loved him back. Even when he got angry with him, he still looked at him with kind eyes. There was an invisible bond between Shio and Takamasa that Katsuya didn't know a thing about.

Just when Katsuya had finally found a place where he felt he belonged, it was disappearing right before his eyes.

* * *

After it got dark, he returned to the condo to find that Takamasa had gone home. He was relieved, because he wasn't sure how he would act if Takamasa were still there. It looked like Shio was in his office, but he came out after hearing Katsuya come home.

"Welcome back," Shio said.

"I'm home..." Katsuya automatically replied.

"Where were you?" Shio asked.

Had he been worried about me? Katsuya wondered. He quietly warned himself not to think about it, and said, "Pachinko."

"Oh, you play pachinko?"

"Just like everyone else did in college. This was the first time since I came here, though." It was an awkward conversation. Katsuya couldn't look Shio in the eyes, and Shio had reverted back to his cold, distant attitude. "Takamasa-san went home?"

"Yeah, finally. He gave you trouble, didn't he, Katsuya?"

He called me Katsuya again! he thought, blushing. "I'm sorry about yesterday. He just wouldn't stop."

"If you give in once, it's all over with him. He thinks if he keeps it up, he'll always get his way. He'll refuse to go home and start insisting that he wants to move in."

"I didn't know that...I meant to tell him it was okay with me, but only if *you* said yes. I guess I didn't make it clear enough."

"It's my fault that I didn't tell you that's how he is. He'll just keep asking the same questions, so it's probably better if you don't get involved anymore."

Katsuya had no intention of doing so, anyway. He had promised himself that. But Katsuya realizing it on his own and hearing it from Shio's mouth were completely different things. Shio had practically looked him in the face and said, "Don't interfere with us."

"I understand." It's not like he wasn't depressed enough already. He had been depressed ever since he had seen them kissing last night. He never wanted to think about it again. Katsuya turned to go to his room.

"Katsuya!" Shio quickly grabbed his arm to stop him.

Surprised, Katsuya turned around, and Shio let go of his hand. Shio looked surprised at his own behavior. "Um, I'm going to make some coffee, can we talk?"

"I'll make it."

"No, let me. You always make it." He made Katsuya sit on the sofa. Shio cheerfully turned on the coffee maker, and before long, the aroma of coffee drifted throughout the room.

He handed Katsuya a mug filled to the brim with coffee.

"Thank you," Katsuya said, and Shio smiled, relieved. He drank the coffee with milk and sugar in it. Holding his cup, Shio sat down beside him. Startled, Katsuya looked up and locked eyes with Shio.

Seeing Katsuya's confused expression, Shio stared at him evenly. "I'm sorry I was so childish yesterday."

"Shio-san..."

"It was Takamasa's fault, yet I blamed you. I'm sorry I acted like that towards you."

Katsuya couldn't think of what to say.

"And not only that. I know you tried to apologize, but I wouldn't even listen. I just want to let you know, you have no reason to apologize." Shio's kind voice echoed in his ears.

Why is he being so nice to me? I'm only his roommate, Katsuya thought.

"It's okay, Shio-san. I understand why you were angry at me."

"Katsuya?"

"Takamasa-san's your brother; he's important to you. You love him with all your heart; I can tell. You couldn't scold him because you love him. So of course you were mad at me."

"...Love him?" Shio seemed confused, but so was Katsuya. He didn't even know what he was saying anymore. He didn't understand why Shio was being so nice to him. It was supposed to be Takamasa who was important to Shio, so he didn't know how to act when Shio treated him so nicely.

"Well, you love him, don't you?" If it was true,

he just wanted to know so he could get it over with. He didn't want to be unsure of the answer anymore.

He remembered the wonderful day they had spent together in Odaiba that Shio had called a date. He had felt like he was floating on air when Shio treated him like that. He told himself he would never have these kinds of expectations again.

"I love him as a brother." Shio gave a safe answer, and seemed a little confused.

Katsuya felt like asking about what he had seen the night before.

"I saw you and Takamasa-san kissing last night."

"What?"

"In the middle of the night, I wanted to apologize, so I went to the living room. Takamasa-san was there, and while you were sleeping, I saw him kiss you."

He knew it. Shio had been sleeping and hadn't realized. He could tell by the surprised look on Shio's face.

"That's..."

"I was shocked. In many ways." But his biggest shock was realizing that he loved Shio so much. The faint longing he had had for him 12 years ago was now transforming into real feelings. He loved Shio. He loved him. But it was true that he was dismayed by those feelings.

"Kissing me? Are you sure that's what you saw?"

"I'm positive," Katsuya asserted.

"But...it was just a kiss," Shio stammered.

"Just a kiss?"

"In some countries, a kiss is just a greeting."

"So Takamasa-san was just greeting you while you were asleep?" Katsuya said harshly. Shio realized how harsh it sounded, too. He looked like he was thinking about something for a while, and then looked at Katsuya's face.

"Is that what you're mad about?"

"I just..."

"You're condemning me because of a stupid kiss?"

"A stupid kiss? Condemning you? Who's condemning who?" Katsuya was so angry, he felt hollow. Having Shio say "just a stupid kiss" bothered him, but maybe he *was* condemning him.

"You're criticizing me right now, aren't you?"

"Criticizing you? What are you talking about?"

"It's okay. Do whatever you want. Say whatever you want. Tell me what's bothering you."

Katsuya stared sadly at Shio.

"I'll listen to everything. So please, don't make that sad face anymore." Shio wrapped both hands around Katsuya's face. Katsuya was stunned as Shio gazed into his eyes. He held his breath. His body stiffened and he couldn't move; Shio was touching his cheeks gently. He couldn't even move his tongue; he just stared up at Shio's beautiful face.

"Takamasa's kiss was nothing. It meant nothing to me. See how easy it is for me to kiss someone?" Shio brought his face close to Katsuya's, his hands still touching Katsuya's cheeks.

It felt like Katsuya was watching it happen to

someone else. He had no idea what Shio was about to do. Before long, Shio's lips touched Katsuya's, and Katsuya came back to himself at the warm sensation. Shio's soft lips nibbled gently at Katsuya's, kissing him slowly.

Ohh...Shio's kissing me...

As soon as he realized that, Katsuya surrendered himself to Shio. It was the first time that he had kissed the person he had been longing for. He was drunk with ecstasy.

Chapter 8

After the night they shared their first kiss, Shio and Katsuya's relationship totally changed. When Takamasa had showed up, Katsuya had been full of confusion and hesitation, but now, he could smile again. He was so sincere and carefree it was almost tiring.

Shio had no idea he would have gotten so much pleasure from just one kiss.

He found himself becoming addicted to Katsuya. He thought Katsuya was so adorable, so precious.

So when they were together, he touched him and kissed him.

Katsuya was shy at first, but eventually, he got used to Shio's sudden kisses, and, as he did, his face shone brightly.

Soon it would be Golden Week, a holiday celebrated nationwide.

Katsuya was going to use his vacation to go home, and Shio decided to accompany him. If he stayed home, Takamasa would just bother him, anyway. Also, he wanted to visit his uncle's grave. As Shio suggested that, Katsuya said excitedly, "If it's okay with you, why don't you stay at my house?" When Shio told him he had planned to stay at his uncle's house, Katsuya looked as disappointed as a child.

But at least he would still be nearby. Shio

suggested that they go around together, and Katsuya cheered up immediately; his face lit up like the sun.

Their week in the country together passed like a dream.

The first two days they each spent with their families and visiting the cemetery. But from the third day onward, they were free to see each other every day.

They visited the fields and parks Katsuya and Kazuki had played at, and the candy store they went to every day. Katsuya showed Shio around, sharing his memories with him fondly.

"That summer was so fun. Even though he was from the city, he wasn't stuck up or anything. We played together every day and got all dirty. I didn't want Kazuki to go back to Tokyo, I wanted him to stay here forever."

"Kazuki didn't want to go home, either. 'I wanna stay with Katsuya!' he would yell. He threw such a fit when he found out he had to come here, but then he also threw a fit when we had to go home!"

Katsuya smiled at Shio's story. "I used to pray to God that Kazuki would never leave. That he wouldn't have to go back to Tokyo, and that he could stay here. If that happened...then Shio-san would have to stay, too," he said, and glanced at Shio.

Shio smiled at him, making Katsuya embarrassed.

"Because I was there, too?"

"Yeah, I liked you so much then. If Kazuki could stay, then you could, too. My childish heart thought so. Do you remember? Every night when it got dark, you'd come get Kazuki. And you'd say to me, 'It's getting late; you should go home.' Then we'd walk down the road together, and I would stare at you the entire way home."

Shio had been a child then, too, and probably hadn't understood the meaning of Katsuya's stare. But he remembered Katsuya well. He was an intelligent, honest child. He had welcomed Kazuki that summer with open arms. He had been a great friend to Kazuki.

"What about now?" Shio asked teasingly. Was he still important to him?

"Now...I still love you. You know that, don't you?" Katsuya stammered.

"Yes, I know." Shio reached out and took Katsuya's hand in his. Katsuya gave a sweet, soft smile at Shio's touch. He squeezed his hand back, and Katsuya gave him an even brighter smile. Shio wanted to kiss him. A sudden desire welled up inside of him.

However, in the country, things moved slowly, so he didn't dare do something so bold there. Even though it was difficult, he suppressed his impulses.

* * *

The week at home passed quickly. They knew that their busy jobs would be waiting for them when they returned to Tokyo.

Katsuya was so busy with work that he forgot all about Takamasa. He hadn't even seen him since the last time. When they got home, there were tons of messages from him for Shio, but Shio never returned the calls.

"Have you talked to Takamasa-san since then?"

The boy still bothered Katsuya a little, even though Takamasa hadn't showed up lately.

"Don't worry about him. He's busy with school. His professors this semester are really strict, so he said he has to study really hard."

"Oh, really?" It still looked as if Katsuya was uneasy.

Well, Katsuya had seen Shio and Takamasa kissing, so he might not be so easily convinced. Maybe Shio was treating the situation too casually.

Ever since he had graduated college, he hadn't had a steady girlfriend, but he had shared his bed with many women. Shio's main concern when dating was to avoid any future troubles, so he tried not to let romantic feelings develop. He preferred having friends with benefits.

He didn't think of Katsuya in the same way, though.

Of course, Katsuya wasn't a woman, so it was wrong to think of him as such. But he felt that Katsuya was precious. He felt intoxicated by Katsuya's kisses, just like he did when he made love to a woman. It's not that he was unpopular with women, but he felt like he had nothing to lose.

"Katsuya." Hearing Shio call his name, Katsuya flew towards him. He was a little taller than Shio, and gazed at him with eyes full of expectation. He had such a straightforward heart, a straightforward gaze. Shio didn't know anyone else like him.

"Shio-san." Katsuya's cheeks blushed slightly as Shio pressed his lips softly against his. He knew the taste, the sweetness of those lips, and he answered Shio by slightly opening his mouth. Shio took that opportunity to slide his tongue inside Katsuya's mouth, in between his teeth, slowly invading his inner mouth.

"Ahhh...Ahhh...Ah..." Katsuya moaned as Shio's tongue roughly pushed against his.

It was strange. When they were like this, it was like they shared something. Something neither of them could see. They drowned in the sweetness of each other's lips. They lost themselves in each other, and the two of them felt like they were melting together, becoming one.

What was this feeling? Shio loved Katsuya. He thought Katsuya was so precious. He had never thought he could love a man. He had thought that when Takamasa had confessed his feelings to him. But now he felt passionate towards Katsuya.

"Shio-san...Shio-san, I love you," Katsuya said passionately between kisses. He grabbed both of Shio's hands, and held them before his eyes like they were some sacred object. He gave him countless solemn kisses on the back of the hand to the tips of his fingers.

It was like a medieval knight giving the princess he loved a kiss to swear an oath. It made Shio's heart swell.

The days passed peacefully. As Katsuya became more used to his job, he became busier. He started to come home later from work.

Shio was also busier lately, after being put in charge of a new consulting job.

In between those busy days, during an evening in

the middle of May, Shio showed up at Katsuya's office.

"Oh, Ozawa-san. Long time no see." A familiar woman from Human Resources greeted him with a smile.

"Yes, it has been a long time. How's business?" He was fairly sure her name was Inada.

She tilted her head as if she wasn't sure. "I heard that there are more registered users in our portal site. I'm not sure about the Sales Department, though. Hatanaka-san and Narita-san are always visiting clients, but it doesn't seem like there have been any really large projects lately. Only small ones."

"Small ones are fine. As small ones accumulate, they become big ones."

"I suppose you're right!"

He glanced towards the Sales Department, but the desks were empty, so it looked like Katsuya hadn't returned yet.

"Is Soga-san here? We have an appointment."

"Yes, he's here. Please go ahead, I'll bring some coffee." The president's door was open, as usual. As Shio walked in, Soga said, "Oh, I've been waiting for you!"

They exchanged small talk, while they waited for Inada to bring in the coffee. When she left, Shio began to talk about the real reason he was here.

"About Ka...Narita-kun's company housing..."

"Oh, it's moving along. It's not ready yet, but it shouldn't be too much longer now."

"About that...he can stay with me from now on."

"Hm?"

"I don't care if he stays. When the company housing is ready, could you just let someone else have it?"

Soga was surprised. When Shio remembered his reaction when this all started, it was no wonder.

"What's this all of the sudden?"

"Oh, nothing, I just think it would be nice if things stayed the way they are now. Narita-kun has finally gotten used to the condo, so I would feel bad if he had to move again." Shio was a little flustered, and Soga laughed heartily.

"Hahaha! So, it looks like you guys hit it off, huh? I'm glad! I was worried, because you usually hate everyone. But I guess everything's okay now."

"Hate...everyone?" He didn't know Soga had been worried about them. It was true that Shio had never liked strangers. It had gotten a little worse after he graduated from college, and it seemed like Soga had been anxious about it.

"Well, that's how Narita-kun is. That's why you probably let down your defenses. Isn't he a good kid? He's so honest and serious. I have high hopes for him."

"Yes, I agree." Shio remembered how good the energetic Soga was at judging the character of others. Lots of former employees of his were thriving at other companies.

Thanking Soga, he excused himself from the president's office. In any case, he no longer felt scared about coming to pick up Katsuya suddenly. Shio felt relieved.

He headed towards the Sales Department and

found Katsuya at his desk.

"Shio-san!" Katsuya said, standing up.

"Good work today. How is everything?"

"Great! I'm doing my best. I've been visiting clients every day. Are you going home now?" Katsuya quickly started to clear off the top of his desk, and Hatanaka stared at him, exasperated. He didn't have to get so excited, even though Shio had come all the way to Katsuya's office to invite him home.

"If you're done, you want to come home with me?" Shio smiled.

"Okay!" Katsuya finished cleaning up his desk, grabbed his jacket and followed Shio. Hatanaka and Inada watched them leave, and then looked at each other with wide eyes.

That night, Shio took Katsuya out to dinner.

They ate at a famous Italian restaurant and slowly savored seasonal dishes. Katsuya liked the red wine Shio ordered for them, and they exchanged small talk while they drank.

In the center of the table there was a glass candle votive, and on the other side of the flickering flames, Katsuya stared at Shio. His gaze felt comfortable. They enjoyed their dinner slowly, and then left the restaurant. They had planned on taking a taxi home, so they started to walk towards the main street. Katsuya murmured, "I want to be with you tonight."

"Katsuya?"

"Shio-san...I want to be with you forever."

Shio's heart pounded. He had thought this day would come. Katsuya was a man, after all. It was natural for him to want to do more than just kiss. However, Shio was confused. He wasn't sure he was ready yet.

"What about you?" Maybe it was from the wine, but Katsuya's eyes were slightly red.

"I..."

"Can't I stay with you?"

Without answering him, Shio raised his hand and hailed a taxi. "Get in," he offered, as if to avoid answering. Katsuya took that as a refusal and bit his lip with a hurt look on his face. He dejectedly got into the car. The taxi took off, and Katsuya looked out the window silently.

Shio grabbed his left hand. He had been quiet, but when Shio squeezed his hand again, Katsuya shyly squeezed his hand back.

* * *

Katsuya's heart raced furiously. Perhaps it was because of the wine they drank at dinner, but Katsuya had blurted out his heart's desire.

He understood why Shio had caught his breath. He had brought it up out of nowhere, no wonder Shio had been surprised. However, Katsuya's feelings had grown stronger that day, and it swelled inside him so much, it had nowhere to go. He was at his limit. He wanted to do more than kiss. He wanted Shio to touch him more. He wanted to get to know Shio better. Everything he didn't know about him. Shio held his hand during the whole taxi ride, and didn't let go of it even when they got out.

Holding each other's hands tightly, they silently

got in the elevator. Did Shio know how he felt? What he wanted to do? Shio remained silent, but he was still gripping Katsuya's hand. The sound of Katsuya's heartbeat echoed in his ears. When they reached the seventh floor, he felt his legs tangle with nervousness. Shio walked quickly, pulling Katsuya along behind him.

Shio suddenly stopped walking. Looking up, Katsuya saw Takamasa standing in front of their door once again.

"Welcome home, Shio-san," Takamasa said, as his gaze turned to Shio and Katsuya's interlaced hands. They quickly let go, but it was too late. Takamasa had definitely seen them holding hands.

"It's late. Go home," Shio said coldly.

Takamasa smiled sadly and nodded. "I will. But first, I have to talk to Narita-san about something."

"To Katsuya?"

"Yeah. It won't take long. I'll go home right after."

"What do you need to talk to him about?" Shio said, suspiciously. He had no idea what Takamasa would need to talk to Katsuya about.

"None of your business! I just want to ask him advice about work, since he just graduated and everything."

Shio still looked doubtful. He unlocked the door and invited Takamasa inside. "Well, I'm going to take a bath. Make it short. When you're done, you need to go home."

"Okay."

Shio was about to leave the living room when Katsuya looked at him as if he didn't want him to leave. There was no way Takamasa really wanted to ask him for advice. He wanted Shio to help him, but all Shio did was nod to him as if to say, "The rest is up to you."

After Shio left the room, Takamasa quickly made himself at home on the sofa. He beckoned Katsuya to sit beside him. As he sat down, Takamasa got straight to the point. "He said to make it quick, so I will. What is your relationship to Shio?"

"Huh?" Katsuya didn't know what to say at such a blunt question.

"I said, what are you to my brother? I saw you holding his hand."

"So this isn't about work?"

"Does it sound like it is? If I didn't make up some excuse, he wouldn't have let me in." Takamasa glared at Katsuya, his eyes full of hostility.

Katsuya was confused, and looked at the door Shio had left from. It didn't seem like he was returning any time soon.

"Narita-san, are you listening?"

"I'm listening. I'm just Shio-san's roommate."

"Roommate?" Takamasa knitted his brows together with amusement.

Katsuya realized exactly what kind of situation he had gotten himself into. He had to tell him the truth. "But, I love Shio-san. A lot," he declared, staring at Takamasa in the face. At this, Takamasa finally showed his true colors.

"Narita-san, you must have misunderstood. Shio

has absolutely no..."

"I haven't misunderstood a thing. I truly believe Shio-san feels the same way."

"Then you're a fool," Takamasa spat out.

That was fine with Katsuya. After all, it had taken 12 whole years for him to realize his feelings. He *was* a fool.

"You don't know the first thing about Shio," Takamasa said viciously.

That was true, but Katsuya was trying to get to know him.

"There will be plenty of time to get to know him," he said. "I'm sure Shio-san will tell me everything."

"Then what about this? The secret he's been keeping. I doubt he'll tell you himself so why don't I tell you?"

Katsuya's heart pounded at the word "secret." A bad feeling pulled through his body. He forgot to breathe.

"A long time ago, Shio had sex with me. He acts like he doesn't remember it, but he did."

Katsuya stared, dumbfounded.

"Do you know why?" Takamasa continued without mercy. "Because the truth is, Shio loves me. But since I'm his brother, he's holding back his feelings. He feels that it's wrong, so he shut his feelings away deep in his heart, and that's why he tries to avoid me. Because he loves me."

"You're lying."

"I'm not lying. If you think I am, ask him yourself. Shio had sex with me. It's a fact. He had sex with me because he loves me. Do you understand? Or, has he had sex with you, too?" Takamasa looked at Katsuya's face, and after he guessed that the answer was no, he laughed loudly. "I thought so. If he loved you, he'd have sex with you. Like he did with me! He doesn't love you. You already know that. He's only nice to you because you're so obedient. Like a pet you'd keep to pass the time."

Takamasa's voice reverberated in Katsuya's ears like a gong.

Katsuya's face went pale, and he clasped his trembling hands together.

Takamasa was lying. He had to be. But what if it was true?

Katsuya couldn't stand the thought of it. He was utterly confused and stunned. All he could do was stare blankly ahead.

Shio finished his shower and returned to the living room. "Are you done talking?" He had changed into pajamas and was drying his hair with a towel. Takamasa turned to him and nodded happily.

"Yes, I'm done. Shio, why are you wearing pajamas? Aren't you going to take me home?"

"I drank alcohol tonight, so I can't. Take the train or a taxi."

"Oh, well. I guess I'll go home now."

"Be careful."

Katsuya felt Shio looking at him, but he couldn't bring himself to look back at him.

"Narita-san, thank you very much. Bye, Shio. Good night," Takamasa said, his voice dripping with insincerity. He exited the living room, leaving Shio and

Katsuya by themselves.

Shio wasn't sure how to react to this strange silence, so he said, "What did he want? He said something about advice?"

Katsuya didn't answer, and silently stood up.

"Katsuya?" Shio asked worriedly, but Katsuya didn't answer him. His whole body told him not to look Shio in the face.

"Katsuya, what's wrong?" Katsuya tried to walk past him but Shio grabbed his arm. Katsuya automatically shook his hand off and silently moved towards his room.

"Katsuya!" Shio followed him. Katsuya knew that Shio had sensed something was wrong, but he leaned his back against the door and refused to let Shio in.

This was his only sanctuary.

He wouldn't let anyone step foot in it.

Tears ran down his cheeks.

But Katsuya didn't even realize it.

Chapter 9

Katsuya had a dream in his light sleep. He was in the field he loved to play in when he was a child. For some reason, Katsuya was in elementary school again. He stood in a familiar place, and there were many of his friends around. When they saw Katsuya, they waved at him and yelled, "Come here!" Seeing his friends greet him so warmly, he jumped right in and began to play.

They ran about the field, not caring that their clothes had become covered in mud.

The primitive smell of the earth. The fresh breeze. He began to forget about all the things that had happened in Tokyo.

While he played, he lost track of time, and the sun began to sink down into the sky. One by one, his friends seemed to disappear.

As evening fell on the park, Katsuya realized that he was all alone. Since he had been left behind, he knew he should go home, but for some reason, he couldn't remember how to get there. He had often played here, yet he couldn't remember how to get to the road home. Katsuya was depressed.

The sky kept getting darker.

What should I do? I can't go home. Uneasiness flooded his chest and Katsuya started to feel frightened. Hugging his knees to his chest, he looked up at the sky. It was slowly getting darker. Just then, he heard the sound of grass crunching behind him. As he turned around, he saw a slender silhouette walking slowly towards him.

It was Shio.

However, it was Shio as he had looked that summer they had spent together; when he was still in junior high.

Shio walked up to the surprised Katsuya, smiled kindly, and held out his hand. "Katsuya. I came to get you. It's late, so let's go home."

Katsuya was silent.

"Come on, let's go home. To our house."

Katsuya kept looking at Shio, but couldn't move. He really wanted to take Shio's outstretched hand and be held against his chest, but he couldn't. He was frozen; all he could do was stare up at Shio's face.

Then he woke up. He leapt out of bed and looked around. Of course, he was in his own quiet room, no one else was there. The faint early morning light peeked through the curtains.

He sluggishly climbed out of bed. He had had trouble sleeping the night before. He kept falling in and out of light sleep, so when he woke up, he didn't feel refreshed at all. His head felt heavy.

He began cooking breakfast as usual, a simple one of toast, ham and eggs. As soon as it was ready, Shio woke up and came in the room. "Katsuya." Shio saw him standing in the kitchen, and came right up to him, peering at his face. "Did something happen with Takamasa?"

"No."

"I know that can't be true. Did he say something to you? What was it?"

"Nothing. It's between him and I. Stay out of it," he forcefully said, without making eye contact.

Shio suppressed whatever he had wanted to say, and sighed tiredly. "Okay, then."

It was the first time Katsuya had ever talked to him like that. Shio became quiet and said nothing further.

It was too painful being all alone in the condo with just Shio, so Katsuya was relieved when he arrived at work. The usual morning sights, the usual familiar faces.

However, the only reason he was relieved was because he had escaped the nervous atmosphere of being with Shio. He knew that running away wouldn't solve his problems. What Takamasa told him the night before was still weighing heavily on his heart. Shio and Takamasa had a relationship. Maybe it was because they weren't real brothers that Takamasa adored Shio so much and was so obsessed with him. If Katsuya were Takamasa, he would probably love Shio, too. He was that charming.

But he had a problem with Shio's part in it. Katsuya had thought Takamasa's obsession had only been one-sided. Thinking about how they interacted with each other, it was hard to believe that they had been involved. He had even believed Shio when he had told him Takamasa's kiss meant nothing to him.

He had been captured by Shio's kisses. He had been so kind, and kissed Katsuya like he was the only one that mattered to him, so he thought that meant that

Shio loved him.

But if he said Takamasa's kiss meant nothing to him, maybe it was the same with Katsuya. Shio had said a kiss was like a greeting to him, so maybe he had just gotten so close to Katsuya that it was just a way of expressing that closeness, and it didn't mean anything at all. Katsuya realized that he was starting to believe what Takamasa had said, and was stunned.

Even though he had accused Takamasa of lying at that time, now he was leaning more towards the idea that it was really true. He wanted to believe it was a lie, but he just couldn't. The main reason was because of his own lack of self-confidence. He wasn't confident that Shio loved him.

The other night, he had gathered up the courage to tell Shio he wanted to be with him. To Katsuya, it was a once in a lifetime confession. But Shio hadn't said anything. All he did was hold his hand. Maybe that was the most considerate thing Shio could have done.

Ahh, stop it! The more he thought about it, the more he lost confidence and got depressed.

He was getting distracted from his work. During a meeting with a client, he paid no attention and was scolded by Hatanaka. Then, he had to draw up some project plans, but they were full of mistakes and he got lectured again. As he apologized, he felt the void grow bigger inside of him. Because of all his mistakes, he had to work late, but he was kind of thankful for it.

He was afraid to go home and face Shio. He might say something to him. He might just completely lose it. He had no idea what he might do, and he was afraid.

* * *

"I'm home."

After work, Shio had dragged his tired body to his parents' house, which he hadn't visited for quite some time.

Takamasa greeted him, looking surprised. "Shio?"

"Where's Mom and Dad?"

"Watching TV in the living room. Why are you...?"

"I have to talk to you. Come to my room." Takamasa looked like he had no idea what Shio was about to say. He bit his lip and stared at Shio. Ignoring him, Shio climbed up the stairs. Shio had left home when he was a senior in college, so his old room had only a bed and a dresser in it. There were no chairs, so he sat on the end of the bed and waited.

Takamasa came in soon after. Closing the door behind him, he said coldly, "What do you want? You never come home anymore, so it must be something important."

"What did you do to Katsuya?" Shio asked as calmly as he could.

"You came all the way here to ask me that? Why didn't you ask him?"

"He won't tell me."

"Then I didn't say anything. Don't worry about it."

"I don't think so. You hurt someone who is very important to me. Of course I'm going to worry about him."

Takamasa froze at the words "very important to me." He stared at Shio in disbelief and then let out a strange laugh. "Shio, don't tell me you're acting this desperate for *that* guy?"

"I am."

"That's not like you. What's wrong with you? You never get this desperate about someone. It makes you look like a fool."

"When someone is important to me, I get desperate for them. Like when you were in the hospital and had to have all those surgeries. And when Kazuki got hurt riding his motorcycle. When someone is important to me, I'll get desperate for them."

"Why were you so desperate for me?" Takamasa asked, his voice trembling. He was already thinking of a comeback when Shio said something he never expected.

"You had surgery and we didn't know whether you would live or die. I prayed desperately for you to survive. Your small body had to withstand so many surgeries. Every time I saw you holding back tears when they stuck you with needles and tubes, I wished that I could change places with you," Shio said shakily.

His little brother had battled illness for so long, and Shio loved him with all his heart. Because he loved him so much, he had turned a blind eye to Takamasa's selfish behavior and forgiven him for his mistakes.

However...

"Takamasa, you remember Akiko, right?" As Shio said her name, Takamasa's face froze with fear. In the back of his mind, Shio enjoyed his reaction, and continued. "I know all about it. What you did to her, what you said to her. I've known all along."

"You're...lying," Takamasa said, his voice shaking. He looked down at his feet.

Shio stared at him. "No, I'm not. I just never told you. I pretended not to know anything. Even when she left me, I knew everything and I still let her go."

"But...why?"

"It wasn't just about you. Things weren't going well between us. I just brought up marriage to try to make things work again. Even if you hadn't done what you did, we would have broken up eventually."

"Well then, why? If you knew what I did, why didn't you say anything?" Takamasa kneeled at Shio's feet and looked up at him searchingly.

At that desperate look, Shio smiled kindly and said, "Because I forgave you, Takamasa. Because you're important to me. So I said nothing, and forgave you."

Takamasa continued to just look at him.

"I truly believed that you'd never do something so stupid again, so I forgave you."

"Shio..."

Shio realized that he had been wrong. By not making Takamasa own up to his mistakes, he had made the same mistake twice. It was partly Shio's fault, too.

Tears poured from Takamasa's eyes. At that moment, he finally realized that he had betrayed his beloved brother's trust. But he still clung to one last hope.

"B-but! I love you! I've always loved only you!"

"I've told you how I feel, too, and I thought

you understood."

"I do! But ever since you let him live with you, you've loved him more than me! You told me you could never love another man, and that you only loved me as a brother. That's why I tried to give up on you! But now you're giving him special treatment!" Takamasa clung to Shio and dug his nails into his shoulder. Tears spilled down his cheeks and dotted Shio's shirt. He cried bitterly, pressing his whole body against him.

Shio gently touched his shoulder and whispered, "I'm sorry."

"Why are you apologizing?" Takamasa's screams made Shio's heart hurt.

"I'm sorry. I love Katsuya." He should have admitted it earlier. He had been hesitant and confused about his feelings, and had ended up hurting both Takamasa and Katsuya.

Seeing the determined look on Shio's face, Takamasa screwed up his face and began sobbing like a child. Shio tightly embraced him just as a mother would, cradling him.

* * *

Katsuya was still working overtime, as he glanced at the clock on the wall. It was almost 10:00 p.m. He hadn't been able to make dinner. He hadn't even contacted Shio to tell him he would be late, so he couldn't relax. He was reluctant to call him on his cell phone. If he called home, there was a chance Shio wasn't there yet, so he tried there. Luckily, he got the answering machine, and left a message, relieved.

"It's Narita. I have to work overtime today, so I'll be late. Tomorrow's my day off, so if I finish up everything here I'm going to a friend's house. So don't worry if I'm not there." Katsuya hung up the phone, and thought, *Why did I lie and say I was going to a friend's house? I only have one friend in Tokyo—Kazuki.*

And he didn't even want to go to Kazuki's house. After all, he was Shio's brother, and was living with his girlfriend in a one-room apartment. If he came over all depressed, it would only bother Kazuki.

Katsuya didn't know what to do. He loved Shio. But in order to clearly tell him his feelings, he knew he should ask Shio himself if what Takamasa had said was true. But he was too scared. What if Shio told Katsuya that Takamasa was the one that he loved? Just imagining that was almost too much for him to bear. If that happened, there was no way he could stay at the condo anymore. His "dormitory" could go screw itself. He would leave that condo and probably just wander around Tokyo in despair.

There weren't very many people left in the office. However, Katsuya wasn't even halfway done with his work. Depressed, he continued working on a project proposal.

"Still at it, huh?" said a voice suddenly above his head. Looking up, he saw President Soga on his way out of the office.

"Yes. Good work today. Are you leaving now?"

"Yeah. I guess you have some overtime, then. If you're the last to leave, make sure to lock up." Waving his hand, the president was about to leave the office when Katsuya remembered something.

"Oh! President! Wait a minute, please!" Soga stopped and turned around. *Yes?* his face seemed to say as he returned to Katsuya's desk.

"President, you said before that Shio-san's condo was just a temporary housing arrangement for me, and that you'd find a proper company housing complex for me, didn't you? I was wondering what was going on with that."

Soga nodded his head, as if he was remembering something. "Oh, well, Ozawa told me to let some other employee use it."

"What? Why did he do that?"

"Oh, didn't he tell you? The other day he came to me and said, 'Narita-kun will be staying with me from now on, so don't worry about the company housing.' So I guess things are going well, huh? He even said he'd begun to think having a roommate was pretty good!"

"Oh, I see..."

"I'm actually thankful for it, myself. Someone else wanted to move into company housing, so now I can give it to him."

"I understand. Thank you for everything." Katsuya bowed his head. Soga raised his hand cheerfully and left the office.

Shio had gone to the trouble to tell the president that he was going to take Katsuya in from now on. He had brought the idea up once before, but he didn't know Shio had talked to the president about it. On one hand, Katsuya felt genuinely happy, but since he couldn't figure out Shio's true intentions right now, he was also confused.

His feelings kept wavering. He loved Shio. He wanted to be with him.

Ever since that summer 12 years ago, he had only wanted him.

But what should he do? The person he longed for was out of reach. He felt far, far away.

In the middle of the silent office, Katsuya clasped his hands together in prayer and closed his eyes. *Please give me courage. Please give me the courage to laugh and smile with the person I love again.*

Chapter 10

There wasn't a cloud in the sky. Next week it would be June, and the heat of the sun was getting stronger in the early summer. Shielding his eyes from the bright sun with his right hand, Katsuya breathed in the salty sea air. It was around lunchtime, and he was relaxing in Odaiba Beach Park. He watched families playing in the sand together, and young people that were windsurfing. Everyone's faces looked so happy. They looked like they were having so much fun. Even though he was watching them from afar, Katsuya felt comforted by them.

Katsuya had ended up staying so late the night before at work that he just laid on the couch in the lounge and had fallen asleep. When he had woken up, he finished his work and left the office without an idea of where he was going. He had left a message that he was going to a friend's house that day, so he didn't return to the condo.

He wandered about town for a while, wondering where he should go. He really didn't feel like going anywhere. Since he came to Tokyo, he had hardly gone out by himself at all, so he didn't know his way around very well. However, his legs had somehow taken him to Odaiba. Odaiba—where Shio had shown him around. That day, they had paid their respects at the temple in

Asakusa and boarded the ferry. He remembered fondly how Shio had smiled and called their outing a date.

This time he boarded the Yurikamome, and, after getting off at the station, had followed the road Shio and he had gone up before.

Everything looked pretty much the same as it had then. But maybe it was Katsuya that had changed.

That spring day, he had spent the day with Shio, and he had thought that their hearts had connected. Ever since that day, he had felt Shio getting closer to him. Even Shio, whom he had once thought of as cold-hearted, had acted like he had felt the same and treated him so kindly.

"No matter what happens, I can't stop loving Shio..." he murmured to himself.

The ocean view stretched out in front of him and his words floated up to the sky.

He loved Shio. Even if what Takamasa had said were true, he couldn't lie about those feelings. Feelings that had continued inside of him for 12 whole years had to be real. *Twelve years...*Katsuya thought. He had spent those 12 years yearning for Shio, but he realized that Shio had spent those 12 years differently. He didn't know anything about what had happened during those years. He didn't know what had happened between Shio and Takamasa. He didn't know what their history was. They shared a bond no one else knew about. Katsuya couldn't come between them.

Katsuya thought back on those 12 years. He had longed for Shio all throughout elementary school and junior high. In high school, he had basically given up on ever seeing Shio again, so he had started dating a classmate. In college, he had sex with a woman for the first time, but it had been sex without love. It had felt empty.

Come to think of it, Shio had said his kiss with Takamasa meant nothing to him, too. A kiss without love means nothing. Sex without love means nothing. Katsuya somehow felt like he understood what Shio had meant when he said that.

He ordered a drink on the cafe terrace inside the park and killed time. After leaving the cafe, he wandered around the promenade, and sat down on the same bench he and Shio had sat on that day.

The sun was starting to sink into the sky.

What should I do tonight? Maybe I should just go home, he thought, but his back felt heavy and he couldn't get up. As he worried about what he should do, the faint pink sky began to get darker and darker. There were a lot of couples on the other benches around him, and he began to feel uncomfortable. He felt like he was getting lost in the darkness, as he looked up at the sky. He felt like a child who had been scolded by his parents and didn't want to go home.

Just then, he heard a voice from behind him.

"Katsuya."

It was a familiar voice.

Turning around, he saw Shio standing there. Katsuya stared at him blankly, and Shio reached out to him.

"I came to get you. Let's go home," he said.

"Ah..." Katsuya hadn't expected to be so surprised.

He looked back and forth from Shio's outstretched hand to his face, utterly confused.

It was just like the dream he had. In the dream, Katsuya had been by himself in the darkness when Shio had come to get him. He was so surprised that his dream had come true that his body froze. Shio put his hand back down. Katsuya was worried that Shio had taken his silence as a refusal, but Shio smiled kindly at him. "Can I sit down?" He pointed at the bench.

Katsuya nodded, and Shio quietly sat down beside him. "How did you know I was here...?"

"I just kind of figured it out. You don't know your way around Tokyo very well yet, so there weren't very many places you could be."

Katsuya didn't know what to say.

"But I'm glad I found you. I have something to tell you."

Katsuya's heart pounded. His throat was suddenly dry as a bone.

Shio watched as Katsuya's face tensed nervously and quietly began to speak. "I talked to Takamasa. About you. We talked about it together. He won't do anything to hurt anyone again. Please forgive him."

"You talked to Takamasa-san?" He was a little surprised. He didn't think Takamasa would tell Shio the truth, of all people. He thought all Takamasa would do was talk back and avoid the issue.

"Not about what he said to you. I already knew, without him having to tell me. Because I knew that he told you something that really hurt you. I knew that he told you something that completely shocked you."

"How do you know if he didn't tell you?"

"Because this is the second time he's done it. Before he did it to you, he did the same thing to a woman I was dating."

Katsuya inadvertently looked into Shio's eyes. Shio smiled sadly at Katsuya's surprised look. "It was a girl I was dating in college. After going out for about three years, we started to not get along very well. I thought it would improve the situation if I proposed to her after we graduated. I told Takamasa about it, and I guess it just triggered something in him. He just couldn't allow it. So he met with her without telling me, and told her everything—the secret between just Takamasa and me."

"Secret..." He gulped. *Could that secret be the same one...?*

"It's true that I had sex with Takamasa once. So, of course, my girlfriend left me. When she did, Takamasa didn't say a word, and I realized what had happened. Just from how my girlfriend and Takamasa had both acted. But even though I knew, I never really blamed him. I had basically driven him to do it, so without saying anything, I just forgave him. I should never have done that."

"So you *did* have sex with him." Takamasa had hurt him deeply the day he told him, but now it felt like he was going to burst. *So it was true. Shio and Takamasa had a physical relationship. Takamasa told the truth, after all,* a spiteful voice said inside Katsuya's head.

Katsuya's face went pale with shock, but Shio was still cool and collected. He recognized his own mistake, and calmly continued. "No matter what I say right now, it'll sound like an excuse. But, when things weren't going well with my girlfriend, I was so worried. I started drinking heavily. I had just started living by myself in the condo, and one night, I came home and Takamasa was there. He was still in high school. He had a fight with his dad and asked if he could spend the night. That's when it happened. I was completely drunk, and I had sex with him."

Katsuya remained silent with shock.

"The next morning, Takamasa confessed his feelings to me. He told me he had always loved me. But I knew that I had made a terrible mistake, and I just couldn't return his feelings. His love bothered me, and I deserted him because of it. I'm sure it was a normal thing for a young boy to feel, but he told me he didn't care even if we just had a physical relationship. So I told him I could never love another man."

"I can't believe it..." Katsuya finally said through his shock.

Shio had kissed Katsuya so many times, and adored him. He never would have thought he had such a fundamental problem. That must mean he couldn't love Katsuya, too. He had always thought so, but Shio had been so kind to him, he had fooled himself. He tried desperately not to cry. There were still many people in Odaiba Park, so he didn't want to cry in front of them.

"Katsuya."

"It's okay. It's okay, Shio-san."

Shio looked at him with a worried look on his face. Katsuya pushed his hand away and turned. "It's okay. I'm sorry. I've been mistaken this whole time. I'm really sorry."

"No, Katsuya. I'm the one who was mistaken."

"No, it's okay. Don't...don't worry about it. I'm sorry I forced my feelings upon you. I'm sorry, I'm sorry." Tears spilled down Katsuya's cheeks, and he quickly raised his hand to wipe them away, when Shio took his hand. He looked up, surprised, and saw Shio looking at him with a serious look on his face.

"Katsuya, listen to me. I was the one who was mistaken. I love you. Do you understand me? I'm in love with you, Katsuya. I finally realized it. You're a man whom I was able to love. I want to prove it to you. I love you more than anyone."

"Shio-san..." Was it his imagination? Shio's beautiful mouth had just said, "I'm in love you, Katsuya." He had confessed his feelings to him for the first time.

"So that's why I came to get you, Katsuya. I wanted to tell you everything. I wanted to ask for your forgiveness. I'm so sorry I made you sad. I'll take responsibility for everything Takamasa has done. Please forgive me. Please forgive me...and let me in." Shio's eyes were wet but peaceful, so Katsuya knew he was being completely genuine. There was a time when those eyes had seemed cold to him. When he had been treated harshly and felt like there was nowhere for him to go.

But...Shio is such a kind person. He squeezed Shio's hand, and Shio smiled broadly at Katsuya's shy reaction.

"Katsuya..."

"I'm so happy you came to get me," he said, his voice cracking. He wasn't sure what he should say.

That's all that would come out. But it looked like his words were more than enough for Shio.

"Of course I came."

"I didn't know where else to go..."

"Oh. Well, let's go home. To *our* house." It was starting to get very dark in Odaiba. The view at night there was called Tokyo's million-dollar view.

However, Katsuya didn't see it at all. All he could look at was Shio's beautiful face gazing only at him.

* * *

Katsuya felt like he was walking on a fluffy cloud, and didn't remember much about what happened after that. They got into Shio's car and headed towards the condo. Shio told him to take a bath so he could relax. After he was done Shio fixed them a simple dinner, which they ate together.

It felt like he was in a dream. Shio had told him he loved him, and they ate a dinner together that Shio had made. If this was a dream, he prayed that he would never wake up.

After they finished cleaning up the kitchen, Shio said, "Go into the bedroom." Katsuya did just as he said and started to walk towards his own room, when Shio caught up with him, smiling.

"Not your bedroom, silly. My bedroom. I'm going to take a bath, so wait for me in there, okay?"

Katsuya's face turned bright red and he walked out of his own room. Of course he was embarrassed at his own misunderstanding, but Shio had just told him he was taking a bath and to wait in his bedroom! He was filled with intense embarrassment.

He entered Shio's bedroom for the first time. On the left-hand side, there was a built-in closet. In the corner, there was a double bed. Maybe it was because his office was in a different area, but his bedroom was simple. There was a nightstand next to his bed with a lamp, watch and car keys on it. "So this is Shio-san's bedroom..."

Leaving Shio's bedroom, he went to the office in the next room. Inside was a desk and bookshelves all in a row. The room somehow felt hard and cold. Just like Shio was when he was working.

After finishing his bath, Shio came to him, wearing a bathrobe. Katsuya panicked because he had come into the office without his permission, and bowed his head saying, "I'm sorry I came in here without..."

But Shio just smiled.

"It's okay. You can use anything in here you like. I have lots of books, so maybe you'll find some of them useful."

"Oh, thank you." Katsuya picked up a book and flipped through the pages. He loved books. His eyes sparkled as he looked at the book in his hand.

Suddenly, Shio's hand plucked the book out of his hand. "You can read later. I want you all to myself right now," he whispered teasingly. Katsuya's whole body flushed. Shio took him by the hand and led him back to his bedroom. He guided him to the bed, and Katsuya obeyed. "I love you." Shio put his arm around him. As he whispered to him, he gave him little kisses on the mouth, and Katsuya closed his eyes, captivated. Shio's tongue pushed into his mouth, and Katsuya hesitantly did the same. Shio enjoyed his reaction, and gave him an even deeper kiss in response.

Holding him close, Shio laid him down on the bed. The sheets were cool; they felt so good. They eased Katsuya's nervousness.

"Katsuya, have you ever done this with another man?" Shio smiled.

"No...because you've always been the only one for me."

"Since when?"

"Twelve years ago, when you came to the country that summer. Ever since then—" Shio didn't let him finish. He was so adorable Shio couldn't stand it, and he began to devour Katsuya's lips noisily.

"Shio-san, Shio-san..." Katsuya moaned in between kisses.

Wrapping his hands around Shio's neck, he kissed him back aggressively. In response, Shio shifted his body slightly, and at the same time Katsuya looked to see what he was doing, he felt Shio's hand sneak into his pajama bottoms. Without hesitation, the hand went into his underwear and grabbed Katsuya's member.

"...Ahhhh...ahh..."

"I'll make you feel so good, Katsuya."

"Shio...san..."

He began to move his hand slowly, but as Katsuya reacted more, he started to jack him off harder and harder. It was so much more stimulating than when Katsuya did it by himself. He felt so much pleasure that his mind went blank; his breath became rough.

At some point, Shio had taken off Katsuya's underwear, and held his bare member in his hands. He unbuttoned his shirt and Shio's tongue began to lick his pink, erect nipples.

"Ahh...Shio-san, Shio-san..." His body trembled. His young body was reaching its limit; he couldn't wait any longer. "Shio-san, I can't stand it anymore...I'm, I'm going to come!"

"Go ahead. This is only the beginning." Shio began to stroke Katsuya roughly, while teasing his nipples with his tongue gently, at the same time. Katsuya's head began to crackle like it was filled with electricity. As soon as he thought he couldn't take it any longer, a tingling feeling raced through his body.

"Ahhh..."

Katsuya soaked Shio's hands, as he collapsed on the bed, exhausted.

"Shio-san..." He laid on the bed for a while, spaced out, breathing heavily. Looking up, he saw Shio lick the semen off his fingers. He turned bright red at the sexiness of the moment. At the same time, he felt himself growing hard again.

Shio noticed the change in Katsuya's body. With a charming smile, he knelt in between his legs and took him into his mouth.

"Mmmm! Shio-san, why are you—"

"I told you I would make you feel good, didn't I? Let me make you feel even better." While Shio's tongue moved while he was talking, a strange sense of pleasure raced through Katsuya. It felt so good. He felt like he

was going crazy. However, he was worried that Shio was
doing something that he didn't want to do.

"But...if you don't want to, you don't have to. Just
with your hand is fine..."

"Who said I didn't want to? You don't need to
worry about that at all. I'm doing it because I want to. I
want to suck your dick, Katsuya."

Katsuya swelled inside Shio's mouth. Hearing
those filthy words come out of Shio's mouth, he
surrendered his body to him.

Katsuya felt bad that he was the only one getting
pleasure. He wanted Shio, too. Shio, whom he had been
longing for all this time. "Then I want to. Let me do it,
too."

When Shio was silent, he clarified, "Let me suck
your...your dick."

"Don't force yourself."

"I'm not! I want to!"

"Then let's do it together." Sitting up, Shio slowly
began to take off his robe. Katsuya watched him, his
eyes full of passion. "I don't have a perfect body like
you, Katsuya. I'm a little embarrassed."

"Don't say that..."

"No, it's true. You have a beautiful body, Katsuya.
It's so beautiful I can't take my eyes off of it." It was the
first time Shio had said he was beautiful. Katsuya smiled
with embarrassment. As he watched Shio take off his
robe, he unconsciously held his breath.

Shio's body was slender and white. It was true
that his body was narrower than Katsuya's, but his
muscles were lean and his figure was well balanced. It

was still very beautiful. "Shio-san, you're so beautiful."

Shio smiled and lay back down with Katsuya. First, he placed his hands on Katsuya's cheeks and slowly intoxicated him with kisses. Then, he kissed his neck, his collarbone, and then slid his mouth over each of his nipples. The sound of his wet kisses filled the room. Shio kissed Katsuya's skin like he was precious. He gave him small kisses everywhere.

"Ah...Shio-san..." Shio's lips reached his hardness yet again. He had only been semi-hard while Shio had been kissing him, but now he was fully erect.

"I'm happy you liked that."

"Shio-san...let me have yours, too." He couldn't express how much pleasure he felt. He could barely speak. His voice was hoarse. Shio turned his body around and held his member up to Katsuya's mouth.

"It's too late now to say you don't want to."

"I won't." He took Shio in both of his hands, handling it slowly. Shio was already rock hard, and he trembled at Katsuya's touch.

"Ahh..." Shio sighed with pleasure. After stroking Shio with his hand, Katsuya began to move his tongue back and forth on him. He sucked on the head first, and then took him in his mouth. As he did so, Shio also took Katsuya in his mouth once again. Their bodies were intertwined as they both devoured each other. If Shio nibbled gently with his teeth, so did Katsuya. If he took him deep in his throat, Katsuya imitated him.

It was as if Shio was teaching Katsuya the ABC's of giving head, and Katsuya obediently complied. If it was possible, he wanted them to both come together, but he was at the mercy of Shio's mouth, and was almost at his limit. In just a few moments, he ejaculated into Shio's mouth. "Shio-san, I'm sorry..." He tried to apologize, but Shio held his body down. Taking Shio back into his mouth, he roughly used his tongue. Before long, Shio came and filled Katsuya's mouth with the semen of the man he loved. He swallowed it thirstily.

They both lay side by side on the bed, breathing heavily. Their heads, fuzzy from pleasure, gradually began to clear. Katsuya began to feel sorry that the passionate moment was about to cool down, and he looked at Shio. He was lying still beside Katsuya, his skin flushed with pleasure.

"You were so good..."

"So were you, Katsuya."

"This is like a dream, doing this with you."

"It's not a dream. We have plenty of time, so we can continue the rest later. I'll be right here, so you can rest now."

What? Katsuya thought, and gazed at Shio's face. "The rest?"

"I want to make love to you, but we shouldn't do everything all at once. We can take lots of time so you can get accustomed to it."

"No, I'm fine. I want to do it now."

"We don't have to rush it. Don't you know that it will hurt?" Shio talked to him like a child, as if Katsuya didn't know anything about having sex with another man.

Katsuya turned his head and said evenly, "I want you, Shio. Right here, right now. If I don't, I'll always be jealous of Takamasa-san."

"Katsuya..."

He knew it was mean to bring up Takamasa. But he felt absolutely desperate. No matter how much time they had, if they didn't do it now it wouldn't mean anything. He wanted Shio so badly. No matter what, he wanted Shio right then and right there. Shio stared at the determined look in Katsuya's eyes and got up. He took something out of the drawer in the nightstand. It was a packet of lotion and a condom. He showed it to Katsuya, which made Katsuya swallow hard.

"Make me want it."

Katsuya tried to draw that same pleasure out of Shio once again. He took Shio's soft member in both hands, and bent over, stroking it passionately. After he got him hard again, he took him in his mouth, and sucked on him, using all the things he had just learned. Obscene slurping noises filled the room. Shio let out a low moan of pleasure.

It seemed like the embers of their passion had ignited again, and Katsuya felt himself getting just as hard as Shio. He wanted to make love to him so bad he was trembling.

"Okay." Shio pushed his hand away. Instructing Katsuya to lie down on the bed, he quietly put the condom on. With his heart pounding, Katsuya gazed at Shio. Squeezing the lotion onto his hand, Shio got between Katsuya's legs that were spread wide open. "I'll try not to make it hurt so much."

But Katsuya didn't care how much it hurt. He would bear anything as long as he could have Shio.

Shio touched a wet finger on to Katsuya's ass. Katsuya jumped at the sudden coldness and trembled, but Shio's finger didn't stop. He slowly opened him up, and pushed his finger in.

Katsuya felt an enormous pressure, and it was hard for him to breathe. All of a sudden, he felt really scared, and he put his hands on Shio's body.

"Breathe out, slowly..." Shio whispered gently.

"Haaaaaa..."

With the help of the lotion, Shio pushed his finger all the way in. He pushed it in and out, and when he felt Katsuya relax a little, he put two fingers in, and then three fingers.

"Ah..." Katsuya wasn't sure if what he was feeling was pain or pleasure. Maybe there wasn't even a word for this strange feeling. It was supposed to be hurting him inside, but instead, some feeling beyond pain was dominating him now.

"I'm going to put it in now." Shio took his fingers out, and Katsuya sighed, relieved. Seizing the opportunity, Shio positioned his body. His hard member pushed carefully into Katsuya's most intimate place, and then he slowly thrust it all the way inside Katsuya.

"Ahhhhh!" Katsuya couldn't bear it so he cried out. It was so much bigger than Shio's fingers. It hurt so much that he felt like he was being torn open. The pain raced from his back all the way to the top of his head.

His body stiffened, and Shio held him tightly to comfort him.

"Just relax. Take deep breaths, just like that...slowly..." Shio's voice sounded far away.

Tears welled up in the corner of Katsuya's eyes, and as he breathed deeply just as Shio told him to, he felt his body relax. The lotion helped a lot.

Shio sensed that Katsuya had relaxed even more, so he started to move inside of him slowly.

As Katsuya felt Shio penetrate him, a twitching pain made him moan. He soon got used to how big it was, and the pain started to dull. A strange feeling began to break out all over his body, and Katsuya unconsciously put his hand over his mouth.

"Ahhh...ahhh, ahhh!"

"You're getting used to it a little, hmm?" Shio whispered. He was breathing roughly. He pounded Katsuya relentlessly like a piston. He reached down and grabbed Katsuya.

"Ahhh...Shio-san...Mmmm, mmmmm..."

"Katsuya, let's come together," Shio whispered.

Shio's movements told Katsuya that the man wanted to take him to the very height of pleasure. He was at the mercy of the violent movements, and Katsuya rubbed Shio's back at the same speed.

"Haa...ahhh!"

They finally reached the climax they had been waiting for, together. They both ejaculated at the same time, and Shio collapsed, exhausted. He buried his face into Katsuya's broad chest and sighed deeply.

Katsuya knew he was no longer alone. He had gone from being Shio's roommate to his lover, and he felt something inside of him change because of it.

Something new would be waiting for him tomorrow. Together with Shio.

Katsuya rubbed Shio's back gently with both hands. The person he had longed for all this time was in his arms, and as he enjoyed the happiness of that moment, he closed his eyes.

END

Afterword

Hello, this is Yuuki Kousaka. You've just finished reading my book, "Sweet Admiration." Did you enjoy it? This time, I tried to change the setting and characters a bit.

However, isn't it good to change things every now and then? That's what I thought when I was writing this story. I made Shio-san, the *seme*, the ultimate pretty boy, and Katsuya, the *uke*, a strong, muscular young man. I didn't want the story to be about the younger man dominating the older man, so I tried to make Katsuya like a sheepish dog. This is the first time I wrote this kind of character, but I had a lot of fun doing it!

No matter how cold Shio-san was to him, Katsuya still wanted to be with him. When his rival threatened him, he would get depressed. While I was watching Katsuya turn out like this, I found myself sympathizing with Shio-san's feelings. I enjoyed his strange personality.

I probably enjoyed it because I love dogs!

This time, Midori Shiina did the illustrations for me. Shio-san turned out so beautifully; I was really happy! Also, Katsuya reminds me of a Shiba-inu, which was nice. However, my favorite is the cover. It's just how I imagined it! I was so excited for the book to come out! So, Shiina-san, thank you very much!

Also, I'd like to thank everyone who read this book. If you have any comments, please let me know! I'm anxious to hear opinions on my new style. Again, thank you very much.

YUUKI KOUSAKA

Every Boss Needs A
HARD
worke
CAGED SLAVE
密室の虜
A Novel
Available Now!
Written by Yuiko Takamu
Illustrated by An Kanae
ISBN:#978-156970-735-7 $8.95
OAKLA PUBLISHING
www.oakla.com
June
junemanga.c
CAGED SLAVE-MISSHITSU NO TORIKO © Yuiko Takamura 2007. All rights reserved.
Original Japanese edition published in 2007 by Oakla Publishing Co., Ltd.

In SPACE, NO ONE
CAN HEAR YOU...
MOAN?
Ai No Kusabi 間の楔
The Space Between
Vol. 1
STRANGER
A novel
Written and illustrated
by Rieko Yoshihara
Volume 1
On SaleNow!
Vol. 1: Stranger ISBN: 978-1-56970-782-1 $8.95
Vol. 2: Destiny ISBN: 978-1-56970-783-8 $8.95
Vol. 3: Nightmare ISBN: 978-1-56970-784-5 $8.95
Vol. 4: Suggestion ISBN: 978-1-56970-785-2 $8.95
Vol. 5: Darkness ISBN: 978-1-56970-786-9 $8.95
June
junemanga.com
AI NO KUSABI VOL. 1 © Rieko Yoshihara. All rights reserved. Original Japanese edition published in 2001 by Seibido Shuppan Co., Ltd.

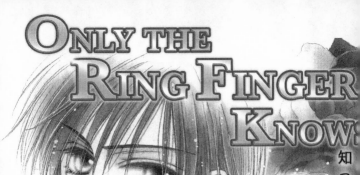

ONLY THE RING FINGER KNOWS

知っている

Two Rings, One Love

The all time best selling yaoi manga returns as a novel

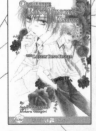

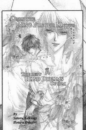

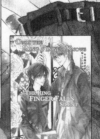

New Novel Series!

by
Satoru Kannagi
Hotaru Odagiri

Text copyright © Satoru Kannagi. Illustrations copyright
© Hotaru Odagiri. All rights reserved. Original Japanese
edition published by TOKUMA SHOTEN PUBLISHING
CO., LTD., Tokyo.

jun